WHAT I LEFT BEHIND

JENNIFER ARCHER

Editor: Archer Editing & Writing Services
http://archereditingandwriting.com

Cover Designed by Sarah Hansen, Okay Creations

Available in eBook & Paperback

eBook ISBN: 978-0-9975991-9-0
Paperback ISBN: 978-1-7358902-0-3

http://www.jenniferarcher.com

AUTHOR NOTE

"What I Left Behind" is a revised and updated version of "The Me I Used To Be" by Jennifer Archer, originally published by Harlequin NeXt.

ACCOLADES

"Archer captures the voices and vulnerabilities of her characters with precision." - Publisher's Weekly

"Archer writes distinctive characters..." - Kirkus Reviews

"...a poignant novel that explores the issues and emotions associated with family, adoption, and love. I found this book to be quite a page-turner, and I did not want to put it down. Archer has a talent for developing interesting, "real" characters, and I was fully engrossed in this novel, which is nicely peppered with humorous anecdotes that add a light-hearted note to the serious topics. I highly recommend this book to fans of women's fiction."- Curled Up With A Good Book (Review of *What I Left Behind* under its previous title *The Me I Used To Be*.)

"...a warm, witty and poignant exploration of some of the most realistically complex, and appealing, characters I've encountered in a long time. Jennifer Archer's prose is lovely without a hint of pretension, never getting in the way of Allyson's narration of her own story. Characters are vulnerable, screwed up and courageous all at the same time, and I loved them for it. Fans of both women's fiction and romance will find a lot to make them happy here." - Karen Templeton, Author of the *Wed In The West Series*. (Review of *What I Left Behind* under its previous title *The Me I Used To Be*.)

"I predicted stardom for Jennifer Archer after reading her first book, and I haven't changed my mind. Every emotion rang true, and even though the novel is told only through the eyes of Ally, the main character, Archer does such a masterful job of showing the emotions of the other characters, you don't realize you're not inside their heads, because you absolutely know what they're thinking and feeling. Highly recommended." - Patricia Kay, USA Today Bestselling Author. (Review of *What I Left Behind* under its previous title *The Me I Used To Be*.)

"...a poignant tale of one woman's road to self-discovery. What she learns along the way is so touchingly emotional you can't put the book down." -- Candace Havens, Bestselling Author of the *Ainsley McGregor Series*. (Review of *What I Left Behind* under its previous title *The Me I Used To Be*.)

PROLOGUE

April 6, 2005

Dear Nick,

If you're reading this, my cancer won and my worst fear of leaving you too soon has come true. I want you to know you were my world, the best thing that ever happened to me, my heartbeat. Raising you has been my greatest joy. I wouldn't trade one second of the past sixteen years!

I hope you will meet life's challenges with courage, grasp opportunities with self-confidence and deal with temptations wisely. Always be true to yourself, Nick. You know what's right for you and what isn't. Learn your boundaries and stay within them.

When you were four, you asked about the "little voice" in your head that warned you were about to do something "bad." I said it was God, guiding you. I still believe that. Trust that voice. When you make a mistake, don't beat yourself up like you're so prone to do. You're human, and humans screw up. Learn from your mistakes, then make changes. That's the key to success.

We've dealt with some of that already. (You know what I'm talking about). You've come a long way, and I'm proud of you.

Nancy and Randy have a place for you until you're old enough to be on your own. Give them a chance. But, if being with them doesn't turn out to be right for you, I want you to look up a woman named Allyson Cole in Portland. She owes me, and I'm trusting what my heart tells me; that she'll want to know and help you. Read my journals and you'll know me better too. Goodbye, my sweet boy. Be happy. I will always be with you.

I love you,
    Mom

CHAPTER ONE

*ix Weeks Later*

I slide a bubbling vegetable pizza from the brick oven, scenting the kitchen's warm air with garlic.

"Allyson?" Joleen, my newest employee, though she's worked here four years, steps up beside me. "There's a lady at the register who wants to say hello."

As Joleen hurries back to work, I set the pizza on the work counter and turn. My heart slides to my toes at the sight of a young woman up front with long auburn hair. But then I realize it isn't this woman Joleen speaks of, but my neighbor Mary Keller, the blonde beside her.

Mary waves and calls, "Hi!"

I smile, wave back, then breathe again.

I've been seeing them everywhere today. On my early morning run before breakfast. In the car next to mine at a light on the way into work. On the sidewalk outside the café when I opened up. Girls and young women with red hair, skin as pale as milk. They're all ages. Gurgling toddlers, gangly, gap-toothed preteens, laughing college students, stressed-out mothers approaching middle age.

Why am I startled each time I catch that flash of color so like autumn leaves? These girls, these women, have stalked me before. Many times. But always, always, each year on this very date. Today of all days, I should expect them.

I've learned only one thing helps drive their image from my mind. Work.

Concentrate, Allyson.

On the aromas of yeast, onion and sweet red pepper, the clatter of pots and pans, the rise and fall of voices and laughter in the adjoining dining room.

Empty your mind.

Get caught up in the rhythm of chopping and spreading, of pouring and slicing.

Behind me, the café hums and buzzes. Today, like all Fridays at the Slender Pea, my gourmet health-food café, the lunch crowd seems noisier than any other day of the week. People are pumped up for the weekend ahead, ready to relax and have fun.

I'm pulling double duty today since Guy Ward, the young man who shares the cooking with me, is off on day five of his weeklong leave of absence. Guy and his wife, Kylie, just had their first child, and he's home getting to know the baby. A girl, by the way. Pink-cheeked, mostly bald and squirmy. A gorgeous, living, breathing doll. And difficult to look at.

At least for me.

Her sparse hair is feathery brown, not red. And though I didn't hold her when I stopped by their house to visit last night, I know exactly how she'd feel tucked in the crook of my arm, a warm, satin weight against my breast. I stared at those tiny fingers, wrapped so tight around Kylie's thumb, and I knew that years from now, when the baby is grown and off living a life of her own, her mother will still feel that gentle grip, that connection.

Work. Concentrate.

When the kitchen wall phone rings for the sixth time, Teena, who is twenty-seven years old and has been with me since I opened the café's doors ten years ago, picks it up as she passes by. "Ally-thon, i'th for you," she says, lisping due to her recent tongue piercing. She presses her palm over the mouthpiece to muffle all the noise. "I'th your thith-ter. Beverly."

As if I don't know my only sister's name. "Tell her I'll call her back when things slow down."

"I can cover for you." Teena jabs the receiver at me. "Here. Joleen hath everything under control out front."

Giving in, though I'd rather not talk to Bev or anyone else right now, I place a second pizza on the work counter behind me. "Thanks. I'll take it in my office. Shout if you need me. And refill the raspberry-tea dispenser, would you?"

I grab a stalk of celery from Teena's hand as I pass by. Seconds later, I collapse in the chair behind my desk and scan the frames lining the opposite wall. There's a magazine photo of me standing in front of the café on the day of the grand opening, certificates proclaiming the Slender Pea Portland's best casual-dining choice for lunch five years running, a newspaper article recounting my "journey to success."

I bite off another chunk of celery, slip on my reading glasses then pick up the phone. "Hey, Bev, what's up?"

"I'm on my break, thank God." As usual, she sounds hurried, dramatic and cynical. All signs that my sister is happy. "After a decade of teaching, my last-period class has me seriously considering a new career."

"Like what?" I ask, knowing she loves her work and would never give it up.

"I'm not sure. Something less stressful. Police work, maybe? Brain surgery?" She sighs. "I was thinking I'd drive over for the weekend and see if you can come up with any better ideas."

My sister lives in Washington. Walla Walla. A long drive away just to cheer me up. I know that's her true reason for wanting to come.

My appetite gone, I throw the rest of the celery stick into the trash. "If you're worried about me being alone tonight, don't be. Warren and I have a date."

"*Good.*" At my mention of Warren, her voice bounces up. Sometimes I think she likes him even more than she likes me. "I hope he has something special planned. You know, to take your mind off things."

Closing my eyes, I picture the silver streaks in Warren's dark, wavy hair, his teasing blue eyes and runner's body. Not bad for fifty-six. Not bad at all. "He doesn't, but I do."

"Please say you're going to tell him you'll marry him."

"*Marry* him?" Shuffling through a stack of mail, I huff a laugh. "He hasn't asked. Not lately, anyway. He finally knows better. I'm happily single and staying that way. Forever."

"Then what's your big plan?"

"I'm going to ask Warren to move in with me."

Beverly sighs again. "Oh, Ally."

"*What?* I think I'm at least ready to take things that far. That is, if he'll agree to live at my place. I worked hard for that house. I finally have it just how I want it. And, no way am I tackling the junk in my attic again."

"I don't understand why two people who want to live together don't get married."

"No marriage, no divorce. What better reason do you need?"

"Great attitude."

"Marriage is just so...I don't know...*permanent*. What if one of these days I decide I want to move to Timbuktu and he doesn't?"

"Ally..."

I don't have to see my sister to know she's rolling her eyes and twirling a lock of silver-gray hair around her forefinger. She's always been jealous of my slow-to-gray brunette hair, while I've always envied her for doing everything right and in the right order. She met the right guy at the right time—after graduating college with honors—married him and raised two great kids—both girls—then went to work teaching school after they both fled the nest.

"Isn't it Warren taking off to Timbuktu that you're really worried about?" she asks. "History's not going to repeat itself, Ally. You won't wake up some morning and find out he's gone."

"How do you *know* that?"

"Because I know Warren. He's not some immature kid. He's a responsible grown-up who loves you."

"It doesn't matter. Him leaving isn't what worries me. That happened a long time ago. And I'm long over it."

"Then, what's the problem?"

Shoving the mail aside, I chew the inside of my cheek. "I don't know. You just make it sound so simple."

"It's not simple, but it's not as difficult as you make it, either." Bev slips into counselor mode, a role she knows well with me for a sister. "Go into a marriage with the mindset you'll work out any differences you face along the way and, chances are, you will."

I want to believe she's right. I want to marry Warren and live happily ever after, to have what Bev has with her husband. Trust. Stability. A love that endures through the bumpy times as well as the smooth ones. But I'm afraid, for me, that fairy-tale existence is not meant to be. "I've never had a good relationship that lasted. Not even with Mom and Dad. Why should this one be an exception?"

"That's not true. I've known you since I was two years old. Our relationship is good, isn't it?"

I laugh. "You got me there. So, you're different."

"And things could be different with Mom and Dad if you'd forgive them. They aren't getting any younger, Ally. They know they handled things badly. They've been beating themselves up over it ever since." Her voice softens. "I'm sorry. I know it's hard. But it's been a long time."

My heart closes off at the mention of my parents and forgiveness in the same breath. *Tough luck,* I think. *Too little, too late.* "Don't start with me about that, Bev. Not today."

For several seconds she doesn't say anything, then asks, "What prompted this decision about Warren?"

I swivel my chair to look out the window. Not a redhaired female in sight on the street beyond. No green eyes boring into me. Accusing, questioning, dismissing. Maybe it's a sign. "It's time I moved on, don't you think?"

"What do you mean?"

My throat knots. "She's thirty-five years old today, Bev. *Thirty-five.* If my daughter wanted to meet me, I would've heard from her by now. I made it easy enough for her to find me. All she has to do is contact the adoption agency. I have to quit waiting for a phone call that'll never come."

A family that will never exist.

"She could still contact you." My sister sounds concerned and as sad and doubtful as I feel. "But you're right that it's time to move on. You've got to quit punishing yourself. Allow some happiness into your life that doesn't involve work." She pauses. "Warren's going to want to get married. You know that, don't you? You can't put him off forever."

"Who knows...maybe some day." I smile. "When I'm older."

Beverly snorts. "Older?"

"Okay, so we can twine rosebuds around my walker for the trip down the aisle."

"*Trip* being the word of concern here. It'd be nice if you married while your vision's still strong enough to see your groom smiling at the end of that aisle."

I cock my head to one side and drum my fingertips on the desktop. "Think about it. Something old, something new, something borrowed, something blue. Warren could be the something old and my hair could be the something blue. Blue-gray, that is."

"Tacky."

As if on cue, Teena pokes her dyed-pink head into the office. "Ally, we have a problem out front."

"Hey! Here's the something I can borrow now. Teena's nose ring. It'll look great with my blue hair."

Scowling, Teena mumbles something about my sanity. "Ally, I'm ther-iouth. You know that little roach problem we're having?"

"Roaches?" Beverly says with disgust. "Did I hear Teena say you've got roaches?"

"Water bugs, not roaches." I scowl at Teena. "And only one. A *tiny* one. When you run a restaurant they go with the territory. They come in with the boxes of food. You just have to stay on top of it."

Teena sniffs. "A cuth-tomer just found our one *water bug* thwimming in hith thoup."

Groaning, I remind myself to call the exterminator again when I hang up. "Tell him no extra charge for the added protein. And lunch is on me."

"No way." Shaking her head, Teena turns to leave. "You tell him."

I groan again. "Gotta go, Bev. I have to see a man about a bug."

After I pop the question to Warren, we decide to skip dinner and go straight to dessert.

He dips a strawberry into the whipped cream, slips it into my mouth then unbuttons the top of my blouse. "Why do you want us to live together, Ally?" His eyes hold mine.

Leaning back against the bed pillows, I swallow the strawberry and reach for his waistband. "Because of your great —" grinning, I grab his belt buckle "—big—" I begin to unfasten it "—*throbbing*—" I slide the belt through the first loop "—heart." Warren chuckles, and I add, "Because we're good together."

He frees the second button of my blouse, his knuckles skimming across the sensitive space between my breasts. "Try again."

I close my eyes, feel the third button release. "Because I'm ready. Because we have fun." *And you made me feel beautiful...*

young...alive. My breath catches as he opens the clasp between my bra cups. "Because I can't stand waking up in the morning without you beside me."

"Not good enough," he mutters just before his lips brush across the top of one breast. "Try again."

Seconds pass in a silence broken only by the sound of his breathing and mine. "Because I love you," I finally whisper.

His head lifts. I open my eyes, and he looks into them, grinning the dimpled grin I adore. "Finally. It took you long enough."

It's true. I love Warren Noble. Funny, fabulous, fifty-six-year-old divorced father of two grown kids. Wonderful conversationalist who challenges me. Skilled surgeon with a great bedside manner both in and out of the hospital. Marathon runner. Owner of magic hands. And my heart. I love him. I'm fifty-two years old and, until now, I've never said those words to any man. Only to a boy of eighteen, and I was sixteen at the time. A girl, not a woman.

Now...after all these years.

It's as if a part of my soul that I've locked away too long has finally been freed. I'm laughing and crying and kissing him, and I can't stop; I don't want to stop.

Warren laughs, too. "Marry me, Ally," he says between kisses.

Oh, God. Bev's psychic. "Warren—"

"I've been waiting a long time."

"Not so long." Only nine months since the first time he asked. Then again three months later. After that, he quit trying.

"It *feels* like forever. We shouldn't just live together, we should make it official. I want the world to know you love me." He places his hands at either side of my face, slides his fingers into my hair, pushing it back. "This sexy, smart, fantastic woman *loves* me. And I love her." Our foreheads touch. "So much. I love you so much, Ally."

His lips taste salty from my tears. Salty and tender and oh, so sweet.

"Will you marry me?" he asks in a voice as quiet and warm as the May night outside my bedroom window.

A *yes* wavers at the tip of my tongue. I'm still terrified, but I know it's the right answer. The only answer. I was crazy to believe we could ever do anything else. "Yes," I say quietly, then laugh and shout, "*Yes!*"

He pulls me into his arms.

"When?" I ask. "Where?"

"This weekend. I don't want to wait and give you a chance to change your mind. We'll fly to Vegas tomorrow afternoon. Hell, we'll fly to Hawaii, if you want, and say our vows barefoot in the sand."

Scooting off the bed, I stand and press my fingers to my mouth, unable to believe this is happening or how excited and crazy young I feel. Like I'm starting over. Like anything's possible. Like everything that's happened in my life was for a reason. To lead me to this place where I belong, to this man, and now I can put the past behind me.

I decide to call Teena and ask her to handle things at the café, then remember I'm catering a bridesmaid luncheon on Sunday afternoon. "Oh, no, honey, I'm sorry." I wince at him. "I can't leave this weekend. We have something going on at the Pea on Sunday. I can't get out of it."

"Can't Teena and Joleen handle things? They won't mind when you tell them you'll be on your honeymoon."

I start pacing. "It's for the mayor's daughter. Her bridesmaid luncheon. I've never left Teena and Joleen and Guy alone to do something so big. This might not be the best event to start with." I bite my lip. "I don't know."

When I pass by him, Warren grabs my hand and tugs me back onto the bed. "Let me convince you." The doorbell rings. He nibbles my neck. "Ignore it."

I wrap my arms around him.

The doorbell rings again. And again.

"Damn," he mutters.

Letting go of him, I lean back. The bell rings a fourth time. "I'll get rid of them."

"Hurry."

I refasten my bra and start to work on the buttons of my blouse as I head through the bedroom and into the living room. The hardwood floors are cool beneath my bare feet. In the entry hall, I flip on the porch light then look through the front-door peephole.

A boy wearing a sweat-stained backward ball cap stands on the other side of the door, staring down at his shoes. I guess his age to be fifteen, sixteen at the most. Here to sell me something for a school fundraiser, most likely. I hope it's that and not one of those poor dropouts who come around peddling magazine subscriptions. I hate seeing kids in that situation, hate turning them away when they look like they're on their last dime. Inevitably, I end up with more subscriptions to add to my ever-growing pile of magazines I'll never have time to read.

I unlock the door and open it just wide enough to peer out. "Hello."

He has a tiny gold loop earring in his left ear. The shaggy tufts of hair curling out beneath the bottom of his cap are light brown.

"Miss Cole?"

Something about the shade and shape of his restless green eyes is familiar. Hauntingly so. "Yes?"

"Allyson Cole?"

I nod. "Can I help you?"

His eyes change, become as hard and cold as emeralds, sending a tiny shock of alarm straight through me. That's when I notice the large duffel bag at his feet. Lifting it, he steps closer to the door and shoots me a cocky grin. "Hello, Grandma," he says. "I'm Nick. Nicholas Pearson."

$\mathcal{H}$er name was Sarah. My baby's name was Sarah. Sarah Pearson.

I hold myself together long enough to feed the ravenous boy —my grandson—the dinner Warren and I didn't get around to eating. Long enough for him to tell me about his mother's death from breast cancer three weeks ago. Long enough to study a snapshot of her standing with Nick when he was much younger, and an older couple—her parents, he says; they died in a car crash four years ago.

While Nick showers and Warren calls Sarah's best friend in Seattle to confirm his story and let her know Nick is okay, I remain as calm as a windless day. I make the bed in the guest room, gather the dirty clothes he tosses outside the bathroom door and take them to the laundry, put away the leftovers and wash the dishes.

Then, when I find him sound asleep in the bed I made for him, I turn off the lamp, walk to my own room...and shatter. Even Warren can't pick up the pieces. Still, he holds me all night while I cry, while I lose myself in memories of the last time I held my child. The powder-clean scent of her head, her wisps of downy hair against my fingers, the soft cushioned pad of each tiny toe. *My baby's dead. My little girl.*

Just before dawn I hear Warren's quiet snores and know he's finally fallen asleep. Slipping from the bed, I creep down the hallway to the guest room.

The boy hasn't changed positions since last night. He's sprawled on his stomach, one arm draped over the spare pillow, the other dangling off the side of the bed. Even in sleep, his jaw is tensed, the hand on the pillow fisted. I wonder why someone so young has so much anger stored up inside of him.

Then it hits me. He's as old as I was when I conceived his mother. Sixteen. That's what he told me when I asked his age.

I sit at the kitchen table in my gown, the photograph of my daughter and her family clasped in my hand. Outside the window over the sink, the early morning sky cradles clouds as swollen as my eyes, as bruised as my heart. I smell rain on the breeze that drifts in.

Sarah.

Her hair is red, like I remembered. The same shade as Sonny's, the boy who was her father. But her eyes aren't slanted and green like his and her son's. Her eyes are big and brown. Like mine.

"We might want to check this out, Ally," Warren says quietly, bringing my head up. He stands in the kitchen doorway wearing only his jeans, watching me. "We should be cautious." He nods at the photo I'm holding. "I don't mean to sound callous, but maybe it's not—"

"It's her." I press my lips together tight as our eyes meet, mine filling for what seems like the thousandth time, his tired and worried and afraid. Afraid for me. I glance down at the photo again, my body racked with sobs. "I know this face," I choke out. "I know her, Warren. I never forgot. Not one single thing about her."

"Ally...oh, honey." He comes to me, takes the photo from my hand, pulls me from the chair then sits and draws me onto his lap.

"I never quit believing that some day she'd come to me, that I'd hold her again and I'd be able to explain why I let her go. I wanted to tell her I never forgot her, I never stopped loving her." I bury my face in his chest. "But I can't. Not now."

I thought I had shed every tear last night, but now they fall again. Warren rocks me in his arms and strokes my hair while I cry. Drained and exhausted, I finally sit back and look at him. "He has Sonny's eyes," I whisper.

Warren doesn't say anything. He pulls a handkerchief from his jeans' pocket and hands it to me.

Pressing it to my nose, I say, "Nick's eyes. They're like his real grandfather's." With a choked laugh, I say, "God, Sonny's a grandfather. I can't even imagine. He's still eighteen in my mind. He'll always be eighteen."

I get up, go to put on the coffee. I've never mentioned Sonny to Warren before. Early in our relationship, I told him about my teenage pregnancy and that I'd placed the baby for adoption. I admitted my conflicted feelings about that decision. He didn't pry for more information. I guess he sensed more than mere conflict in me when I spoke about that part of my past, that he recognized it as a wound that never healed. He said if I ever wanted to talk more about it, he'd listen. And he did. The one time I opened up to him, I only spoke of the baby, not Sonny. Warren didn't ask any questions and hasn't since.

But, he knows when the wound aches. On Sarah's birthday.

Holidays. Times when we're out together, I see a little girl with her coloring and my mood changes. Even then, he never pries. Instead, he does little things, offers simple, endearing gestures of kindness to help me wade through the depression that always ensues, to pull me out of the past and back into the present. Our life together.

The aroma of fresh coffee blends with the rain-scented air. I wait for the pot to fill then pour two cups, add creamer to mine, leave Warren's black. I carry both to the table and sit across from him.

Steam drifts from the cup and warms my face. After several sips, I start talking. "When Sonny and I met, I was a junior in high school. He had already graduated and was working construction to earn money to go to trade school." I puff out my cheeks, release a long breath, then smile. "My parents couldn't stand him. It was the same old clichéd teenage love story you've heard a thousand times before. He wasn't good enough for the professor's daughter. He wasn't smart enough or ambitious enough and on and on."

Warren must hear the old bitterness creep into my voice. He covers my hand with his on the tabletop and gives me a nod of encouragement to continue.

"I was a wild thing then."

His brows lift above his teasing eyes. "That hasn't changed."

"Not like that." I make a face at him. "I wasn't promiscuous, although that's pretty amazing when I think about it now, considering all the parties I went to. There was a lot of drinking. A lot of pot-smoking and more. And I was starting to dabble in all of it. The pot most of all." I shrug. "It was California at the end of the sixties, what can I say?"

He squeezes my fingers. "I lived through it, too."

"Sonny and I and three of our friends took my Ford Tempo, or I should say my dad's Tempo he bought for me to drive to school, and we took off to Woodstock."

Warren widens his eyes and leans forward. "No kidding? *The* Woodstock? You were there?"

"No kidding. I knew my parents would kill me when I came back, or that I'd wish I was dead by the time they finished punishing me, but I didn't care. I was stupid back then. I didn't consider consequences."

"So, you were a typical teenager."

"After we got there..." My voice drifts off. I close my eyes. "That Friday night was the first time. Not just with Sonny, my first time with anyone."

A deep rumble of thunder sounds. Opening my eyes, I glance toward the window where the storm's first drops bead against the panes. "And it was raining..."

The first sprinkles fell at midnight into the dark rolling sea of people. We were only five drops of water in that ocean. Sonny and me. Our friends Chuck, Karla and Dale.

Ravi Shankar played on the main stage and the strains of his mystical sitar swirled around us. I breathed them in, lulled by their magic, my eyelids two velvet weights, my body light and swaying.

After a long drive across country from California and a day and night spent stuck in a ten-mile traffic jam, we had arrived at the festival site on foot that morning. We parked the Tempo on a side road miles away. When I left it, so many other cars, buses and people swarmed the area that I worried we wouldn't be able to find it again. My father would be furious if something happened to that car. Of course, he'd be furious with me anyway for sneaking out and taking off across country with Sonny. And when he found out I'd quit my summer job early to do it...I couldn't even imagine his wrath.

But now the music played and I didn't worry anymore. About anything. I was too caught up in the spirit of half a million strangers united for a weekend of peace, freedom and the best music ever.

"Let's go to the tent." Sonny pushed damp hair away from his face as the rain picked up and I shivered against him.

Chuck turned to us. "Bring back a couple of blankets."

"It might be a while," Sonny told him. "I need some sleep."

His lie made me smile. I knew Sonny wasn't the least bit sleepy, that he only wanted to be alone with me for a while.

"Sleep tomorrow during the day when the bands aren't playing." Karla blinked bleary eyes at us. "You'll miss Joan Baez."

Chuck nudged her and winked. "I don't think it's really sleep he's after."

Grinning at Sonny, Dale added, "We'll leave you alone, man."

I hugged Sonny tighter. "We'll be asleep. Come in when you've had enough. You won't bother us." But I knew they wouldn't leave the music for a long time, that Sonny and I would have the tent to ourselves.

"Sure thing," they said in unison as we turned to leave. "Whatever you say. We'll give you an hour."

"Make it two," Sonny called over his shoulder.

Their laughter followed us as we pushed our way through the crowd.

Sonny laughed, too. "Have you ever seen so many freaks in one place in your life? What did you think of those naked Frisbee players this afternoon? I could've done without those guys."

"I notice you don't say that about the girls."

"I'm only human, Al."

I punched his arm.

"What?" Scowling, he grabbed me in a bear hug, making me squeal.

The sweet scent of marijuana hung so heavy in the air even the rain couldn't wash it away. Like the music, I breathed it in. I wanted to lie down with Sonny beside me and listen to the patter of drops on the tent's canvas roof, hear it mixing with the song's lilting notes.

"I thought Richie Havens was never gonna get to quit playing," Sonny continued. "He was something, man, wasn't he? Staying on until that helicopter showed up with another band?"

He flicked his lighter as we ducked beneath the tent flap to five sleeping bags spread across the floor. Tumbling in and shaking off the rain, we kicked off our shoes, stripped out of our damp jeans and T-shirts then slipped into Sonny's bag wearing only our underwear.

Without the lighter's flame, the tent was pitch-dark. I knew that night was the night, and I was ready; I wasn't afraid. Maybe the joint I'd shared with Sonny and our friends a half hour before gave me courage. Or maybe it was Sonny. How safe he felt, how right, with his body pressed against mine while the rain tapped above us and Ravi's Indian music weaved through my mind.

My head lay on his chest, and I could hear his heartbeat, each breath he drew. I matched my breathing to his. In...out. In...out. Two halves of one soul, incomplete without the other. Nothing could separate us. That's what I believed.

Still, I sensed his mind drifting miles away from me, from us. He seemed sad, lost. No longer the talkative, laughing, live-for-the-moment guy of just moments before. "What are you thinking about?" I asked.

"All that land we passed coming in. Miles and miles with no buildings, just pastures and trees. Man." A long breath rushed out of him. "And the sky, it's so blue. And clean. The farmer who owns this field, I heard he runs a dairy." Another sigh. "I'd like to see it, wouldn't *you? All those fat cows? I wonder if he has horses, too? Christ, I love horses."*

I tickled his stomach. "Why do you want to be an electrician? You should do something with animals. You're good with them." I thought of how my father's German shepherd always ran to Sonny, tongue hanging out, eager for his touch. How the sound of Sonny's voice calmed the dog when nothing else could. "Shep growls at everyone except you. He likes you better than anyone, even Daddy."

"I bet that sticks in Professor Harold's craw." Sonny grew quiet a moment before asking, "So, how could I make a living with animals?"

"Lots of ways. Be a veterinarian."

"You know what it costs to go to vet school? I don't have the grades to get in, anyway."

"Be a farmer, then. Or a rancher. Or both. You could do it." I poked him in the side. "I know you could. You can do whatever you want."

"I'm glad you believe that. My folks sure don't. They gave up on me a long time ago." For a minute, neither of us spoke, just listened to our own thoughts, the rain, the music outside. Then, Sonny said, "A farmer or a rancher, huh?" He tickled me, and I laughed. "I could dig that."

He stilled, drifting again. Thinking. Too much thinking. Too serious all of a sudden. I shifted, then rolled on top of him, my waist-long hair falling around us like a curtain.

Sonny slipped his fingers into it. "What do you see in your future, Al? Tell me."

It didn't matter that I couldn't see him in the darkness. I easily imagined his long, shaggy hair, the color of a weathered copper penny, spread across the bag beneath his head, his narrow green eyes with their distinctive slanting squint that always made them appear to be smiling. "Us together," I said. "A little white house with a big red barn behind it. A farmhouse. Or a ranch house, maybe. Whatever you decide. A pasture with cows and horses. Oh, and squawking chickens in the yard and a great big horny rooster chasing them around."

"You sure that's not me chasing you around?" Lowering one hand, he fluttered his fingertips up my side, scattering goose bumps across my flesh. "What else?"

I touched his head. "Red-haired, green-eyed babies."

One of his hands rested at the small of my back, so warm. The other pressed my head down to kiss him. He tasted of smoke and cheap wine. "Tell me more," he murmured against my lips. "This time just about you, not us. What are your dreams?"

"You're my dream, Sonny." I blinked back sudden tears. Didn't he understand? Didn't he feel the same way I did? "You, the babies, the horny rooster, all of it."

"That all sounds amazing, but you're smart. You wouldn't be happy stuck out in the middle of nowhere with nothing to do. What do you want just for you?"

I'd misunderstood him before; that's what I told myself. He wanted us to have a life together, but one that included both of our dreams. I stroked down to his chin where three days' growth of whiskers brushed prickly soft against the tips of my fingers. "Well, before we buy the farm—"

"Or ranch—"

"Or ranch," I echoed, giggling, "I'd like to go to college. Get a Master's degree, maybe even a Ph.D. Then I want my own business. While you're milking or branding, I could grow the biggest, fattest pumpkins and zucchini and kumquats in the county."

He snickered. "Kumquats?"

"Why not?" I asked, smiling into the darkness. "I could bake pies and sell it all from my own farmer's market. Allyson Cole's Colossal Kumquat Stand."

Sonny made an amused sound of disbelief. "Sorry, Al. Somehow I just can't picture you as Mrs. Old MacDonald."

"How about Mrs. Sonny McGraw, instead?" Neither of us spoke for a minute, then I said, "I want to prove Dad wrong."

"You don't have to prove anything. You're perfect like you are."

"To you, maybe, but he's different. I have to show him I can accomplish whatever I want. Even if . . ."

"Even if I'm along for the ride," Sonny broke in, finishing for me. "You can say it. I know how your old man feels about me."

Overhead, the rain riddled the tent like gunfire. I didn't want my father's bad vibes to damage the weekend fun, the night, our time together.

"Forget him." I touched my lips to his again. "Forget him, Sonny."

"I love you, Al," he whispered, pushing my hair from my face.

The urgency in his tone, the sudden tightening of his arms around me – like he thought I might slip away from him – sent a shiver of both longing and unexpected fear up my spine. "I love you, too."

And then, whether Sonny did or not, I did forget. Everything. Only the drum of raindrops on the canvas existed, the floating music and constant hum of voices outside, Sonny's strong, thin body as he switched our positions and moved over me. His hands and mouth everywhere... everywhere.

"Jesus Christ, look at that. There's a freakin' stream running behind the tent."

I awoke a short time later to the sound of Dale's frantic voice outside.

Karla giggled. "This mud's as slippery as ice."

"Feels more like pig shit," Chuck said. "Hold on to me."

When I opened my eyes, the inside of the tent was still cave-dark. I heard the flap open.

"Get your ass up, Sonny," Dale shouted. "You, too, Ally. We better dig a trench or your little love nest is gonna be knee-deep in water before dawn."

We threw on our clothes and joined them outside.

The rain fell in sheets now. The sea of people churned beneath it. A singer named Melanie was at the microphone. Her gentle voice poured from the stage and, suddenly, tens of thousands of tiny lights flickered on the dark waves as the fans lit flames and lifted them skyward...

I glance away from the window and meet Warren's tender gaze. "I can't explain how I could've felt so happy when the physical conditions were so miserable. All I'd had to eat since we arrived that morning was a cold hot dog on a stale hamburger bun."

"Sounds delicious."

"I think they'd planned on less than half the number of kids that actually showed up. Then the traffic jams kept delivery trucks from getting through to resupply the concessions. I was cold and drenched and hungry, but there wasn't anywhere else I would've rather been. God, I was such a silly romantic." I shake my head and laugh my disbelief at the girl I was.

Warren's eyes hold a teasing glint. "You a romantic? I can't imagine that."

"You don't think I am?"

"Not anymore. Now, you're just a sex fiend." He grins. "I'm not complaining, by the way."

I smile at him then close my eyes. "If I hadn't gotten pregnant, that time with Sonny wouldn't mean anything. It would just be a fond memory. A high school fling."

A floorboard squeaks. Warren and I turn to see Nick enter the kitchen. My heart vaults to my throat. I wonder how long he's been standing beyond the door? I hope he didn't hear what I said about Sonny.

Nick is bare-chested and so tall and thin I see the jutting curve of each rib above his drawstring pajama pants. I think of Sonny again. They're built alike.

My heart knocks against my chest as I push back my chair and stand. "Good morning, Nick."

He pauses just short of the table, nods and blinks sleepy eyes that refuse to meet mine. "Hey." His Adam's apple shifts, and a flush of pink explodes in his cheeks.

"Would you like some breakfast?" I hurry around the table toward the counter, my hands as fluttery as my breath. After opening the refrigerator, I poke my head inside. "I could scramble some eggs. Or do you like them fried? Or pancakes. I could make pancakes or waffles if you'd rather have those. Or French toast. Do you like French toast?" I move a tub of butter aside to reach the juice pitcher, then shoulder the refrigerator door closed, move to the cabinet and take out a glass.

On my way back to the table, I feel Warren's eyes on me and sense his concern over my babbling. Why am I so nervous? Why? He's only a boy. My grandson.

Dear God. My grandson.

"Have a seat," Warren says to Nick in a calm voice, motioning to the chair at the end of the table while I pour the juice.

Nick hesitates before taking the offered chair.

"Does any of that sound good to you?" Warren asks him. "Eggs? Pancakes?"

Nick shifts his gaze from his hands on the tabletop, to

Warren, up to me, back to his hands. I look, too, and am startled to see that he has my long, thin fingers, that our nails are shaped the same. "Just cereal's fine."

"I don't have cereal." All at once I feel ridiculously inadequate, as if I should have been prepared. Had a pantry stocked with Apple Jacks, Frosted Flakes and Froot Loops in case a grandchild I never dreamed existed showed up on my doorstep one night and stayed over. Like I should have expected such a disruption in my oh-so-organized life.

"Eggs, then," Nick says. "Scrambled."

Back at the refrigerator, I take out the egg carton, milk and salsa, grated cheese. "Scrambled eggs. Coming right up." Cheerfulness, as unconvincing as it is phony, raises my voice an octave.

"You're in for a treat, Nick. Allyson's eggs are like none you've ever tasted. She's a chef. She owns her own restaurant. The woman can make canned green beans taste gourmet."

Rattling cookware punctuates the silence that follow's Warren's compliment.

"So, Nick." Warren clears his throat. "We were all tired last night, you especially. Understandably so after that bus ride from Seattle. We didn't finish our talk. Tell us about your dad."

I pause in my egg beating and look toward the table, the whisk poised in my hand.

"I don't have a dad. I don't have any family now." Nick leans back and crosses his arms. When he nods at me, the defiance returns to those green eyes so like Sonny's. "Only her."

My breath catches. I resume beating the eggs, pour them into the heated pan, open the spice cabinet.

"So you're living with your mother's best friend?" Warren continues. "The woman I called last night?"

"Yeah. Nancy Pacheco and her asshole husband Randy. They got custody. I *was* living with them, but not anymore."

Uneasiness settles in the pit of my stomach as I salt and pepper the eggs then pop two slices of bread into the toaster. "I take it you don't like them," I say, stating the obvious.

"Nancy's okay, but I'm just in her way. She has three little kids. I'll take my chances on the street before I go back there. Even a foster home would be better." *Or you.* He doesn't say it; nevertheless, I hear the statement, a plea in his voice.

When everything's ready, I put the food on a tray and set it in front of him. I sit across from Warren, watching as Nick props his forearms on the table and shovels the food into his mouth like he hasn't eaten in weeks.

Ever since he arrived, I've noticed he's always moving. Tapping a foot, drumming his palms on the table or on his thighs. Have boys his age always been so fidgety? Was Sonny? I don't remember that about him. Of course, Sonny was eighteen when I knew him, and stoned as often as not, which mellowed him, I suppose.

Studying Nick, I feel my age for the first time. Fifty-two. Not just a number, a state of mind. Too young to be a grandmother to a sixteen-year-old, at least if I'd done things the right way. And too old to remember what it *feels* like to be sixteen. Or maybe I don't want to remember. I've never married, never had any other children after Sarah. What do I know about raising a teenager?

Panic sweeps through me at the thought of him staying. "I could go with you to talk to the Pachecos, Nick. I'd be happy to do that. You only spent three weeks with them. Maybe you and Randy just need more time to find your way with one another."

Nick shoves the tray away, leans back and crosses his arms. "I'm not going back."

"Your mother must have thought they were the best people to raise you if she couldn't. She must have trusted them to do right by you."

"She didn't have any other choice."

"But—"

"I'm not living with some fucking asshole who orders me around all the time and thinks I'm a pain."

Warren's chin lifts. "Watch your mouth, Nick."

"It's okay, Warren." Anger at Randy Pacheco, a man I don't even know, rises up in me as I fold my forearms on the table and lean in closer to Nick. "Mr. Pacheco said that to you?"

"He didn't have to say it. I can tell. That's why I'm here. Mom left me a note." He lifts his glass and drains the juice in three noisy gulps. "It said if I didn't like living with them I should look you up." Wiping his mouth with the back of one hand, Nick nods at me. "Mom said you owed her."

His words slap the breath from my lungs. Blinking, I stare down at the remnants of food on his tray. *I owe my daughter.*

It's true.

A part of me wants to hear everything else she thought about me, another part isn't sure I could bear to.

"I'm pretty sure she said that because you dumped her when she was a baby," Nick adds, the statement slapping me a second time. "Her journal says she found you through the adoption agency but she never could get up her nerve to contact you."

I lean back in the chair, sick inside, trembling.

Before I realize he's left his place at the table, Warren's behind me, his hands on my shoulders. "Allyson didn't dump your mother, Nick. She—"

29

"Gave her away to someone else. Same difference."

I reach up to grip Warren's hand. "Let me explain."

"What's to explain? You gave her away. My mom *kept* me. Even though the guy who got her pregnant hit the road when he found out. She had to struggle for everything we had."

He scans my beautiful, newly remodeled kitchen and, just for a second, his tough façade slips. Behind it, I glimpse a flicker of raw grief. Vulnerability. "You may have all this, but you didn't have my mother," he says in a choked voice. "And she didn't have anything. Only me."

CHAPTER THREE

*A*t eight-thirty, Warren leaves to make hospital rounds, and Nick wanders around the house and into the garage looking at my things. All the while, he asks curt, impersonal questions I can't answer. How many gigs on my computer's hard drive? Does my stereo sound system run DTS movies? How much horsepower does my BMW have?

After half an hour, I leave him in front of the television and make a call to Teena to tell her I'm running late. She'll have to handle things for a bit without me, which I hate all the more since Guy is out, too. She doesn't sound half as concerned about it as I am.

When I return to the den, Nick's stretched out and sleeping again. Grief exhaustion; I know the signs. Thirty-five years ago, I grieved over losing Sarah and, before that, Sonny. Like Nick, I couldn't get enough sleep.

I'm just out of the shower, a towel wrapped around my head and wearing only a terry-cloth robe, when I go to check on Nick again and hear a quiet knock at the door. A peek through the peephole reveals Beverly outside on my porch. All five feet and one inch of her. I can only imagine one reason she'd make the four-hour drive and show up unannounced so early in the day. Something wrong with Mom or Dad. Despite all the issues between my parents and me, my heart flips over.

Turning the lock, I swing the door wide. "Has something happened?"

"I'll say." She wraps her arms around me and the purse on her shoulder digs into my side. "Warren called last night. He was so worried about you." Tears thicken her voice. She steps back, takes my hands and looks up at me. "Tell me about Nick."

"Come in and see for yourself. He's asleep, though. On the sofa."

"I'll wait. I don't want to wake him."

"Come talk to me while I get ready, then."

She follows me into my bedroom, glancing toward the sofa when we pass by the den. Only Nick's body is visible from the hallway; a throw pillow covers his head, his arms clasped over it.

Bev sits on my bed while I comb my hair. "How are you, Ally?"

"I keep thinking I'll wake up soon, that this isn't real." I watch her in the mirror.

"I'm so sorry about Sarah." Her eyes fill.

My daughter's name hangs in the air between us, as soft and elusive as a dream, the answer to just one of the many questions that have haunted me for so long. Sarah. A beautiful name for a beautiful woman. I didn't name her when she was born. I thought it would make it easier for me to move on. But it didn't make it any easier. Nothing I did, nothing anyone did, helped me forget the pain of leaving her.

I turn away from the dresser, pull Sarah's photograph from my robe pocket, the one of her with Nick and her adoptive parents. Nick hasn't asked for it back yet, and I can't bear not to have it close by. Handing the photo to Beverly, I say, "She's pretty, isn't she?"

Bev studies the photo for several long seconds then looks at me with misty eyes. "She's incredible. I'm so glad Nick found you, Ally. He's your chance to know her."

Nodding, I blink back fresh tears.

My sister glances toward the door. "What's he like?"

"Tall and skinny. Green eyes." Our gazes lock, and I know she's remembering that Sonny looked the same. "His hair's light brown. I don't know where that came from. His father, I guess. It's shaggy and too long. He needs a good cut."

Laughing, Bev twirls a lock of her own hair around her forefinger. "Listen to you. You sound like Mom and Dad did when they used to complain about the boyfriends we dragged home."

I tuck my lower lip between my teeth. She's right. And the last people I want to sound like, or *be* like, are my parents. "He has freckles across his nose. Faint ones, but—"

"Ally, what is he *like?*"

I sit beside her on the bed, hug myself. "I haven't really had much time to get to know him yet, but my first impression?" My sigh sounds fragile, even to me. "Scared and confused. Mad at the world. Mad at me. Cocky and rebellious, at least on the surface."

"He's like you were at sixteen."

She doesn't have to add, *after Sonny disappeared.* We both know that's when my outlook on everything changed. When *I* changed. "I'm not sure I want to remember all those chaotic emotions, you know? Being with him brings it all back, though, like it or not."

"What are you going to do?"

I stare at my lap, afraid to make the wrong decision for Nick. For myself. "I'm thinking of calling the Pachecos, the people who took him in, but I'm not sure."

"Call them about what?"

"Unless there's some reason why it's out of the question, I thought maybe he could spend the summer with me. He could bus tables at the Pea, and we could get to know each other." I look up at her. "What do you think I should do?"

"Trust your gut."

"Okay, then." I nod. "If the Pachecos are fine with it, he'll spend the summer here. After that, we'll see how he feels about staying."

"How you both feel, you mean."

I already know how I feel. Afraid. Unprepared. Unsure of myself. As selfish as it sounds, my life isn't geared toward raising a teen. "I'm not sure I have the right to put conditions on it. When your girls were difficult, you and Dennis didn't cast them out to live with strangers. They're your girls. You worked through it and did what was best for them, not what was easiest for you."

"You're the stranger, Ally, not the Pachecos. You gave his mother up for adoption," Bev says gently. "The Pachecos have custody, not you."

"He's my flesh and blood. I have to try." *I owe my daughter that much.*

She smiles as she reaches up and tugs my hair. "I know you'll do fine."

When Bev returns the photo to me, I stroke my finger across Sarah's image.

"I almost forgot," she says, sounding brighter. "What happened with Warren? Did you ask him to move in?"

"Yes, as a matter of fact."

"And he said...?"

"He said he wanted to get married, just like you told me he would."

Bev looks smug. "What did *you* say?"

"Yes."

She shrieks before I can add, *and then the doorbell rang.*

I call Teena again and tell her I won't see her until lunch. Beverly is my excuse for playing hooky.

My sister and Nick have an instant rapport, and I discover a jealous streak in me I didn't know existed.

"You like video games, Nick?" Bev asks him, as they sit side by side on the sofa and he flips from one television station to the next.

"Yeah. I play them all the time."

"What's your favorite?" Before he can answer, my sister holds up a hand. "No, let me guess." She rattles off two titles as foreign to me as the Japanese alphabet.

Nick stops flipping channels, turns to her and stares. A sudden smile lights his face—a real, full-fledged smile, no sneer behind it. "Both of those. How'd you know?"

Bev breathes on her knuckles then polishes them against her chest. "It's one of my many gifts. One look at a person, and *voila*! I know their taste in video games."

Nick's mouth twitches. "Those two games are like movies. The animation's awesome."

As they delve into a discussion of Xbox versus Game Boy, I remind myself that Bev's life has revolved around children. Raising her own, volunteering at their schools, P.T.A. and Scouts. And now she teaches middle school. The woman knows kidspeak; I don't have a clue.

While Nick and Bev continue to get acquainted, I call the Pachecos. Nancy is friendly enough, but sounds harried and weary. I hear her kids in the background and, throughout our conversation, she has to excuse herself repeatedly to referee squabbles and intercept potential carpet disasters. Her relief is palpable when I tell her I want Nick to stay with me for the summer, which only increases my anxiety. I'd hoped he was mistaken about the Pachecos not wanting him around, but after talking to Nancy, my instincts tell me Nick isn't wrong. Or even exaggerating the situation.

After the phone call, I can't bring myself to think beyond the summer, can't begin to imagine him staying with me longer than three months. With my career, my habits, my lifestyle, making such a situation work seems too far-fetched even to consider.

Nick didn't bring many clothes and forgot to pack his toothbrush, so I suggest we head for the pharmacy then the mall, a place I usually avoid. That's when I discover that Bev doesn't know everything about teen boys. After years of shopping with her daughters when they were Nick's age, she prepares me for hours of him trying on jeans, T-shirts and running shoes while we pace the store.

But we soon discover that sixteen-year-old boys are allergic to clothes shopping.

"There's the fitting room," I tell him, pointing toward a wall of curtains after he chooses a couple pairs of jeans and three T-shirts identical in style, but different colors—dark gray, light gray and black.

He starts for the checkout. "They're my size. They'll fit."

Exchanging baffled frowns, Bev and I follow behind him. "Where's the fire?" she asks him. "I'm out of breath trying to keep up with you."

He glances back. "I'm ready to leave."

"Okay," I say. "Where next? You need some shorts. A jacket, too. And what about shoes?"

He gets in line and turns to me, lifting the stack in his hands. "This is good."

Less than forty-five minutes after we arrived at the mall, we're back in the car and heading out of the parking lot. Neither of us, Nick nor I, mentions what my buying these clothes—and him letting me—might mean. That I'm willing for him to stay here; that he *wants* to stay.

We head for an early lunch at the Pea. I want to eat before the Saturday rush then call the florist to make sure the centerpieces will be ready for the bridesmaid luncheon tomorrow.

The familiar smells when we enter the café make my mouth water, and I realize how hungry I am.

Joleen's readying the register for customers when we walk in. "Hey, Allyson." She grins at my sister. "How are you, Beverly?" Noticing Nick, she nods a greeting at him.

In the open kitchen behind the buffet line, Teena peeks into one of the ovens at a steaming pan of something.

"Smells good," I say.

Teena's spiky pink hair is clasped back on one side with a

black flower barrette. She looks over her shoulder and smiles, and I catch a glimpse of the gold stud in her tongue. "Hawaiian tofu poth-ta. Want thome?" she asks. "The thpinach ravioli might be ready, too."

I notice Bev's bemused and baffled expression and whisper, "She just pierced her tongue. I hear it's some kind of sexual thing."

Teena approaches, holding the huge pan in an oven-mitted hand. "What'ya been up to, Bev? Bethides kidnapping Ally, I mean."

"Same as always. Reading, writing and arithmetic." Bev arches a brow and points into her own mouth. "What about you, Teen? Explain that to me. Is it something sexual?"

When Nick clears his throat, I nudge my sister with an elbow. He's been so quiet, I guess she forgot he was with us. Or maybe talking about sex in front of him doesn't make her uncomfortable. She was always pretty open with her girls when they were his age.

Teena looks aghast. *"Thex-ual?*Who told you that?"

Bev shifts her finger toward me.

"I knew you had a dirty mind, Allython," Teena grumbles.

"It doesn't mean anything," Nick says.

The sudden sound of his voice is so startling, we all turn and stare at him with shocked expressions, as if he just emerged from a coma.

"I know lots of kids with pierced tongues."

I wince. "Kids *your* age?"

"Yeah. Why not?"

"*Why* would be the more logical question," Bev says.

"It must hurt like crazy getting it done," I add.

Bev smirks. "I'm betting heavy drugs are involved. And/or

boatloads of alcohol. Which would explain the decision to do it in the first place. You'd have to be loaded to think stabbing a foreign object into your tongue is a good idea."

Teena blushes beet-red, and I glance at Nick, ready to change the subject. "You like tofu?"

He shrugs. "I've never had it."

"Trust me." Bev wrinkles her nose. "You want the spinach ravioli."

"Ravioli then," Teena says and takes off for the kitchen. She returns carrying another large pan, which she places onto the buffet line.

Joleen, who is twenty and as plain-Jane and low-key as Teena is flamboyant and wild at heart, closes the register drawer then turns and leans against it.

I see questions in both of their eyes as they look from me to the sullen boy at my side.

"This is Nick," I tell them. Shifting to look at him, I explain, "Teena and Joleen have worked for me for years. They're like family." At once, I realize I said the wrong thing, a hurtful thing. Nick's eyes harden again, and I know what he must think; how could I have deserted my own daughter, then made a family with these two girls who were strangers? It doesn't make sense. Not even to me.

"Are you Beverly's grandson, Nick?" Joleen asks. Her thick glasses have slid to the tip of her nose and she shoves them back into place.

"I'm his grandmother, not Bev." Again, the words slip out before I can stop them, before I consider how they might affect Nick. Does he think of me in that role? Probably not. I certainly don't. The woman in the photograph was his grandmother. She looked like a soft, plump, afghan-knitting, rocking-chair grandmother. The rosy-cheeked stereotypical kind you read about in children's books. Nothing at all like me.

Nick's gaze darts to mine then away. A sudden burst of pink stains his cheeks.

Teena blinks liner-smudged eyes and says, "Oh."

Joleen stares at me through her wire-rimmed glasses. "You have the best grandmother, Nick," she finally declares. "Ally took me under her wing during a really tough time in my life. Teena, too."

I wish she hadn't shared that information. Nick radiates negative energy my way. I feel it sizzling.

I don't explain anything more to the girls about him; there'll be plenty of time for that later. "How about some salad and bread to go with the pasta?" I raise my brows at Teena.

"Oh," she says again, still blinking at me as she backs toward the kitchen. "The thalad. Right."

We fill our plates and choose a table. Since it's eleven-thirty, Joleen unlocks the door for customers. It doesn't take long before they trickle in.

Joleen calls me aside as she approaches our table. "I wish you'd talk to Teena," she says in a voice just above a whisper.

"What's wrong?"

"She's getting another tattoo."

From the corner of my eye, I see Nick pause and look at us, his soft drink in his hand. I smile at Joleen and shake my head. "Oh, well. What's one more?"

"But she wants this one on her *boob*. A tiny rose. She wears a double-D cup, Ally. What's that little flower gonna look like when she's old and saggy?"

"A long-stemmed rose?"

Nick coughs. Bev shrieks a laugh.

Joleen's sigh brims with exasperation. "I thought you'd be her voice of reason. She looks up to you."

I pat her shoulder. "I learned a long time ago that once Teena makes up her mind to do something, there's no talking her out of it."

I glance at Nick. He doesn't look back at me, but I notice a spasm at the corner of his mouth before he lifts his fork to eat. He must approve of my spinach ravioli recipe. He shovels it in as fast as he did this morning's eggs and toast. Coal into a burning furnace.

Why can't he just let go and laugh with me? Why can't we have the same instant connection I had with Teena and Joleen? They came into my life, lost and broke and alone, much like him. I gave them jobs, an ear for their troubles, acceptance. It was so easy to do. Why does this feel so different?

With another pat of reassurance to Joleen's back, I return to my chair. "I was wondering if you might like to work for me this summer, Nick?" I stab a cucumber slice.

He looks up, his fork paused midway to his mouth. "Here?"

"You could bus tables. Unload boxes. Lots of things."

He takes the bite, returning his attention to his plate. "Where would I stay?"

My heart twists. Bev smiles, but any fool cann see her heart aches, too. "With me," I say. "You'd stay with me."

Nick takes a drink and shrugs. "Sure. I'd do that."

"Good!" I clap my hands together, wishing I felt as enthusiastic as I sound. "Good." I clear my throat. "Nick, what I said to Teena and Joleen…about being your grandmother?" He still refuses to meet my gaze. His plate's almost empty; I wonder what he'll concentrate on when he's out of food. "I hope that didn't offend you."

"You don't look like a grandmother," he says between chews. "Not like the ones I know, anyway."

Beverly huffs. "Disgusting, isn't it? Tall, skinny little thing. If she wasn't so stinkin' nice, I'd have to hate her." When Joleen walks by again, Bev stops her. "Any chance I could get a slice of pie for dessert? The kind made with real, old-fashioned, bad-for-you sugar?"

"Here?" Joleen scowls. "You know your sister better than that."

Sitting back, I let the reality of what I just set in motion sink in. I'm going to be a grandmother, at least for the summer. Responsible for the care and guidance of this boy beside me. A boy who exists, in part, because of Sonny and me.

And one rainy, muddy weekend a long time ago.

Beverly and I stand in my driveway beside her Tahoe, just the two of us. Though this morning's rain shower was short, clouds still crowd the sky. Across the street, two young men do yard work. One pushes a mower, the other maneuvers a Weed Eater along a gently curving flower bed that borders my neighbor's tri-level house.

Bev refuses to spend the night. After our long afternoon of shopping with Nick to buy things for his room, she says she wants her own bed.

As for the shopping, I'm afraid I went overboard. I could've easily planned a trip to Seattle to bring back his stuff and spared my pocketbook, but I was possessed with this driving urge to spend money on him. And so, I did. A lot. Nick, I discovered, is less resistant to toy shopping than he is to clothes shopping. He chose an Xbox video-game player, a computer, an MP3 player with earphones, new CDs for the old player he brought from Seattle, a pair of in-line skates.

"You can't buy the boy's love, Ally," Bev says to me now.

"I'm not trying to."

"His forgiveness, then. Not that I can figure out what he blames you for."

"For dumping his mother, as he put it." I turn away from her, breathe in the scent of freshly cut grass. "God, will I ever stop crying?"

Her fingertips are soft against my forearm. "Nick's in a lot of pain over Sarah's death. He needs to take it out on someone. You're a convenient target, that's all."

Sighing, I reach for her, and we embrace. "Thanks for coming. Today was so much easier with you here."

"I wanted to be here."

We end the hug, look at one another, laugh and hug again. "I love you," I say.

"That's good, 'cause I love you, too."

I clear my throat. "I'm scared."

"You're going to be fine. Both of you." She opens the door and climbs into the Tahoe. "I'll call every day to check on you."

"I'm counting on it."

I watch her drive away.

Ever since Warren and I started to get serious, we've had dinner together almost every night of the week when he's not working. Lately, most of those dinners take place at my house, and he stays over. Tonight I cook a light meal for the three of us.

As we sit around the table, Nick's as quiet as ever. Warren and I try to ease the strain with pleasant but awkward conversation but Nick reddens when asked questions about his school and friends. His guarded eyes slide to ours then away. I wonder how on earth I'll ever be able to get him to open up to me, how I'll keep him occupied for an entire summer.

After the dishes are washed, I pace before the sofa where Warren sips his wine. "I don't know what to do with him."

Diana Krall's sultry voice fills the den, singing "Besame Mucho." If not for Nick being down the hallway in his room doing who-knows-what, Warren and I would probably be making out by now.

"You don't have to keep him entertained, Ally. Leave him alone some. He'll find his way."

"Or get into trouble." I cross my arms.

Warren sets his wine aside. "It's the same for every kid. And every parent. This is new for both of you. Give yourself some time to get used to the situation. Give Nick some time."

Antsy, I glance toward the hallway. "I'd better go check on him."

Warren shakes his head and reaches for the newspaper as I leave the room.

Nick's bedroom door is closed. Hard music blares from the speakers of the computer I bought him today. I hesitate before knocking.

"Come in."

I open the door and the smell of burning tobacco assaults me. "You need anything?"

"I'm okay."

Nick's stretched out on his back on the bed, a thick, leather-bound book clasped in one hand, a cigarette in the other. The nightstand lamp casts a muted glow in the room. Beside it sits a pack of cigarettes and a Waterford bowl from my dining room buffet that he's using as an ashtray.

"I don't allow smoking in the house, Nick," I say over the music. "Especially in bed. You could fall asleep and burn down the house and us along with it. Besides, it stinks and it's bad for you."

Looking straight at me, he takes another drag, a deep, slow one that he holds in his lungs a long time before blowing out the smoke. Then he reaches over and smashes the cigarette out in my crystal bowl. The butt smolders. So do his eyes.

His behavior confuses and scares me. At dinner he was awkward, blushing and vulnerable. Now, less than an hour later, he's rigid, cold and as impenetrable as an iceberg.

I gesture at the book. "I see you're a reader. Anything good?"

"One of my mom's journals." He closes it.

For the first time, I wish he *would* look away and not pierce me with those squinting green eyes. "It's good that she kept them. And that she left them for you."

"She writes about you."

A familiar hollow ache returns to the pit of my stomach. I nod at the journal. "Maybe you'd share it with me sometime."

"Maybe."

"I'd be honored."

I back from the room and start to close the door then pause. *He's a sixteen-year-old kid,* I tell myself. *I won't let him get to me.* But, the truth is, he already has. Still, if we're going to make this work, I can't let him know how afraid I am of screwing things up and making him hate me. Of failing him. Failing Sarah. If I let him intimidate me, allow him to push me around with those eyes and that attitude, I'm sunk.

"Nick?" When he doesn't look up from the journal, I walk to the computer and twist the speaker knob to turn down the music's volume.

Raising his head, he watches me cross to his bed.

I lift the Waterford bowl from the nightstand then pick up the cigarette pack and place it in the bowl. "I'm serious—I won't have these in my house."

"Fine. I'll smoke outside." He reaches for the bowl, but I'm too quick.

I start from the room. "You're underage, and it's against the law."

"You expect me to sit, stay and obey because you tossed me a few treats? I'm not one of your strays like those girls at your restaurant."

Shaking inside, I pause at the door to draw several deep breaths. Why is he here? What does he want from me? Not my friendship; that much is obvious. "I'm not your enemy, Nick."

"Whatever." He turns onto his side away from me, grabs the sheet and tugs it up to his chin.

Back in the den, I toss the pack into Warren's lap then sink onto the sofa beside him. "Got a light?"

He scowls at me. "You're kidding. You? Smoke?"

"I did in another life and, right now, I'm tempted."

Warren smiles sympathetically at my frustrated joke.

Crossing my arms, I sit back and listen to Diana croon about lost love. "What if I can't do this? Nick needs things I'm not sure I can give."

"Do you want to do it?"

"Yes." I hesitate a moment then turn to him. "No...God, I don't know. It's not something I planned on or even imagined.

In my mind, a grown woman always showed up on my doorstep, not a troubled teenage boy who still needs raising."

"You're not obligated to him, Ally."

"That's what Bev said."

"You could still be part of his life and he a part of yours if he's living in Seattle with the Pachecos."

"You know Nick hates Randy Pacheco."

"Sometimes I hated my dad when I was sixteen."

I shove him gently. "Rudy? How could you hate that sweet old man? He's a teddy bear."

"Exactly. See? Randy Pacheco isn't necessarily an ogre because Nick's at odds with him. He might be the best thing for the boy."

I sigh. "I have to try."

"Because you feel guilty."

"That's part of it."

Warren stares at me several seconds then says, "Well, whatever you decide, you know I'm behind you." He draws me into his arms and kisses me. "We have some unfinished business from last night." Reaching into his pocket, he pulls out a small velvet box and offers it to me. "I love you, Ally."

Emotions well up in me as I take the box and flip the lid. With all the craziness since Nick arrived, I've barely had a second to think about Warren's proposal last night. Or my acceptance. "Oh, Warren." It's perfect. Simple. Gorgeous. A square-cut diamond in a platinum band. "How did you know this is exactly what I would've chosen?"

"I know you." He slips the ring from the box, slides it onto my finger and looks up at me. If he'd never once told me he loved me, I'd know it now by his expression.

I glance at my finger again, watch the diamond sparkle in

the lamplight. Then I kiss him, slow and deep, with all my heart, trying to block out all the whispered doubts that once again crowd my mind.

"Let's go to bed and continue what we started last night," Warren murmurs against my lips.

I pull back, scoot away from him. "Warren...I don't think we should."

Laughing, he grabs my arm and tugs me toward him, trapping me in a hug. "Why not? It's a little late to be shy, don't you think?"

I glance down the hallway toward Nick's bedroom. "Things are different now. I'm a grandmother."

He nips at my ear. "You were a grandmother all the other times we did it, too, we just didn't know it."

"We know it now. *You* know it." I close my eyes. "God, I feel so old."

His deep chuckle shoots a shiver up my spine. "When I look at you, I don't see a grandmother. I see a very sexy woman who happens to turn me on." A low sound of pleasure rumbles from his throat as his hands slide down to my butt. "Especially when you wear that little, black—"

"Warren—" I flatten my palms against his chest.

With a frustrated sigh, he lets go of me and leans forward with his elbows propped on his thighs. "Why can't we just explain to Nick that we're engaged? I doubt he'll give it a second thought that I sleep over. Kids don't think anything of it these days. Besides, if he hadn't shown up last night we'd be on our honeymoon right now."

"What makes you so sure?" I smirk at him. "I told you I couldn't leave. I have that luncheon to cater tomorrow, remember?"

"And I was about to convince you otherwise." He smirks back. "Don't think I wouldn't have."

"Pretty sure of yourself, aren't you?"

"Yeah, I am." His expression becomes serious. "Nick being here doesn't have to change things between us."

"Our relationship's going to change. There's no getting around it. Especially if he stays permanently. I didn't take in a stray puppy, Warren. He's a boy. My grandchild. His needs take priority. That's the way it has to be."

"I understand, and I admire you for it. But Nick doesn't have to be your *only* priority. You have needs, too. And so do I. We can do this together. If you decide he should stay, we can be a family. I'm fine with that."

I study the sparkling ring on my finger. I can't bear the thought of Warren looking into my eyes and recognizing what's churning behind them. So much uncertainty and fear. So many doubts.

"You do *want* me to be a part of this, don't you, Ally?"

I don't answer fast enough; when I look up, I see his hurt expression. "Yes. Of course, I do. It's just—" I sigh. "Don't you think it's odd that on the very night I finally agree to marry you and move on, just *minutes* after I say 'yes', my past shows up at the door?"

"What are you saying? That Nick is some kind of sign? A reminder not to get too close to anyone?"

"Isn't that how it seems?"

Warren shakes his head, runs a hand through his hair. "That's ridiculous."

I cross my arms. The rational part of me knows he's right. But emotionally, I can't ignore what seems like more than a coincidence.

"So, what now?" Warren blinks at me. "The marriage is off?"

"No, just—"

"Just what? Postponed indefinitely?"

"Twenty-four hours ago I found out I have a grandson. I have to learn to be a grandmother before I can concentrate on learning to be a wife."

Warren watches me for several long seconds before pushing to his feet. "Good night, Allyson." He starts for the door.

I stand, too, and follow him. "Warren—"

On the stereo, Diana belts out, "Cry Me a River." I feel like I could. A big, wide, raging one.

"I'll call you tomorrow." He doesn't look back.

I glance at my hand through blurry eyes. "Do you want this back?" I say, my voice choked. "The ring?"

He pauses with his hand on the doorknob. "Do you want to give it to me?"

"No." I shake my head. "No, I don't."

Looking at me over his shoulder, he says, "Then I don't want it. I love you. If you need time to adjust to all this, I understand, and I'll wait for you. But if what you're really doing is using Nick as an excuse to give in to your fear of commitment, that's another story." He holds my gaze, a mix of worry, frustration and affection on his face. "I won't wait forever while you debate if fate sent you some kind of warning not to risk your heart."

When Warren is gone, I sink onto the couch. Is that what I'm doing? Using Nick as an excuse not to face my fears and move on? To finally have the life with Warren that, deep down, I know is right for me?

CHAPTER FOUR

"*Good morning...it's a new day...*"

Grace Slick's voice rang out from the microphone as Jefferson Airplane began to play outside our tent.

Beneath me, the sleeping bag felt damp and smelled of mildew. Sonny had spread a second bag on top of us the night before. Now he spooned me from behind, his stomach against my back, his arm and one leg draped over me.

"Man, I'm hungry." Nuzzling his face into the side of my neck, he laughed and muttered, "I might just have to eat you up, Al."

I giggled. "How can you think about food? The smell in here has killed my appetite."

"That your feet stinkin' up the place, Dale?" Sonny called out.

"It's the mud you're smelling. Dale's at the medical tent." Chuck sounded groggy and as hoarse as a toad. "Me and Karla took him in the middle of the night. He drank some of that electric Kool-Aid going around and started screaming about spiders."

Sonny shifted. "Stupid son of a bitch."

"Hey, man, he was thirsty. He didn't know it was spiked."

"I lost a shoe in the mud and cut my toe getting him over there,"

Karla piped in, yawning. "The nurse made me sit with my foot in a big bowl of stuff. Burned like crazy. She gave me a pair of sandals somebody left, though."

I winced. "Will Dale be okay?"

"The nurse said he would."

Sonny flattened his palm against my growling belly. "No appetite, huh? We've gotta find something to eat today besides those peanut-butter sandwiches they've been handing out. Maybe we should just split."

"We can't!" I rolled to face him. "We have another day." I thought of what awaited me back home. "I'm not ready to leave."

"This is no place for you, Al," Sonny whispered. "I shouldn't have talked you into coming here."

"You didn't talk me into anything. I wanted to."

"It was my idea, though. I don't know what I was thinking. No decent food, no place to pee, all these people tripping on bad acid. What if it'd been you that drank that Kool-Aid?"

"I'm okay. Really, Sonny. I'm having a blast. The music, the people all helping each other, you and me together. It's magic. I'm glad we're here."

"Man..." Worry and frustration weighted his sigh. "Maybe your old man's right about me. I'm stupid and no good for you."

I bristled. "Daddy said that to you?"

"He doesn't have to say it. It's obvious that's what he thinks." He turned his head, so I couldn't see his face. "You could get sick out here, Al. Catch pneumonia or something in all this rain. You could cut your foot like Karla and get an infection."

"None of that's going to happen."

"It might. We shouldn't risk it."

I sat up. "You're just ready to leave, so you're saying anything to get your way."

Sonny rolled onto his back, his hands linked behind his head. "This place has turned into a freakin' disaster area. It's a mess out there. You just don't want to go back and face Professor Harold, so you're gonna argue with me till you wear me out and I give up. Even though you know I'm right."

"You always think you're right."

"And you're as stubborn as your old man, even though you bitch about him."

Across the tent, Chuck blurted a laugh. "Jesus. Lighten up, man."

"Shhh," I whispered, stretching out beside Sonny again, stroking his brow. "Let's not fight. What's wrong? Why are you so worried?" It wasn't like him. "Forget about my dad. Think about us. Just us."

"I am thinking about us. I'm thinking about you, Al. You deserve better."

"Better than what? You're not making sense."

"Better than...Never mind. It doesn't matter."

The quiet anguish in his voice scared me. He hadn't been himself all weekend. Only for short periods of time. Moments when he seemed to forget whatever troubles darkened his mind. Then he'd be Sonny again, laughing and singing, teasing and loving me.

I heard Chuck moving about, felt him step over us. He raised the tent flap, letting soft morning light, the noise of thousands of conversations and the music flow in. A drum-beat started, intensified, pounding...pounding...pounding...

The sound of throbbing bass jerks me awake. I sit straight up in bed. The clock on my nightstand glows 2:00 a.m. Outside in the driveway I hear a car idling and the muffled thump of rock-and-roll music.

Yesterday, while I ran laps at the gym, Nick made a friend on the basketball court; a tattered, shifty-eyed kid named Cameron who dropped by the house this evening after dinner. They stood in the driveway and talked while I peeked out the window every five minutes. I was taking a potty break from spying when Nick stuck his head into the house and yelled, "Be back later!" By the time I pulled up my pants and stumbled to the front door, he and the guy had gone.

I switch on the lamp and throw on my robe.

Nick's been with me a week, and we've made little to no progress toward getting to know one another. At breakfast each morning, I talk. Nick nods, grunts and answers my questions with single, monotone syllables. We're always at the Slender Pea by eight. Nick works quietly, busing tables, washing dishes in back. He follows directions and never complains. Before the lunch crowd arrives, we stop to grab something to eat then get back to work. He's good with the customers, a fact that surprises me. Sometimes, while he's busing tables, I glance over and see him chatting and laughing with someone. The sight gives me hope, but it hurts, too. He's never laughed like that with me. And the only smile I ever receive from him is one laced with defiance.

Each evening, by five-thirty or six, we head for the gym. So that Nick can shoot baskets, I've started running my laps around the indoor track there, instead of outside around my neighborhood. He usually ends up playing a game with anyone who shows up on the court. Then we go home, where our dinner conversation repeats the one we had at breakfast.

Afterward, Nick shuts himself in his room for the rest of the night, listening to music and playing on his computer—so much for the items I purchased in an attempt to win him over. I admit it; Bev was right about that. Rather than buying his love, though, I provided him with the means to entertain himself while shutting me out completely.

The only bright spot in my week was when Warren came by the evening after he gave me the ring to apologize for "overreacting." When Nick went to bed, Warren and I made up. And it was nice. Though I felt a bit inhibited with my grandson in the house.

I'm waiting on the sofa in the dark when Nick closes and locks the front door then tiptoes through the den, headed for his room.

"Hello, Nicholas."

"Shit!" He jumps, faces me. "You scared me."

I turn on the lamp and take a breath. *Cigarette smoke.* I draw another breath, this time through my mouth. "Where have you been?"

"Out with Cameron."

Are his words slurred, or is suspicion playing havoc with my imagination. "Out where?"

His bloodshot eyes shutter. "Driving around."

"Doing what?"

"Jeez. Just driving around. We met up with some people."

I count to five. Slowly. "It's good you're making friends, Nick, but I'd like to get to know them a little better before you take off in their car."

He pulls a small plastic bottle of eyedrops from his pocket and screws off the lid. "I'm not in elementary school."

"I don't care how old you are. You just don't run off without giving me some idea of where you're going and when you'll be back."

All at once, I flash back in time to another wee-hour-of-the-morning confrontation. I was the teenager sneaking in with bloodshot eyes and those same words came from my mother's mouth. I can't believe I've become her carbon copy. At least tonight.

Nick tilts back his head, brings the bottle to his left eye, squeezes out a couple of drops then shifts to the other eye. "I'm going to bed."

"You'll have an eleven-thirty curfew the rest of the summer," I call after him. My mother's words again. I cringe.

*"Eleven—*whatever."

"Okay, midnight. That's fair, isn't it?"

His bedroom door closes.

"Good job, Allyson," I mutter. "Fantastic."

Few challenges I've tackled in the past felt as overwhelming as dealing with Nick does now. Certainly not putting myself through college, grad school and culinary school by waiting tables. Not paying my rent, during that time, without a dime from my parents. Stacked against those, Nick wins first prize at making me crazy.

Just after dawn, I call Warren. "I can't do this."

He yawns. "What happened?"

"Nick refuses to talk to me. He's starting to make friends but he avoids introducing them to me. He still sneaks smokes in his bedroom; it stinks like an ashtray in there. He plays music too loud and he spends too much time on the computer." I take a breath. "Shall I go on?"

"There's more?"

With the phone pressed to my ear, I wander into the

bathroom and turn on the water in the tub, hoping a warm bath will calm me. "He didn't get home until two o'clock this morning. I didn't know where he went, and he didn't call to let me know he'd be so late. I'm not sure, but when he finally came in, I think he'd been drinking or smoking pot. Maybe both."

Warren blows out a noisy breath. "Wow."

"I'm not cut out for this, Warren. It's good that I gave Sarah up. I don't have the parenting gene."

"Like I said before, you have to give yourself time. I'll help you. I raised two of my own. I have on-the-job experience."

I breathe in the steam that rises from the filling tub. "That's just it—you've *raised* your kids. You shouldn't have to deal with all this crap. You and Marjorie were lucky Reid and Annie didn't put you through this sort of thing."

"Oh, really? Did I ever tell you about the summer before Reid's senior year? We were so proud of him. He made his midnight curfew every night, sometimes he even got in early. He'd come to let us know he was home, and he was always stone-cold sober. Then one day the guy mowing our yard told me I had a cut window screen. Reid's window. He'd been coming home at curfew then sneaking out again."

I bite back a laugh. Warren's son is in medical school now, and he's so serious and focused it's difficult imagining him ever being the least bit wild.

"Then there's sweet, innocent-eyed Annie," Warren continues, on a roll. "The first weekend of her freshman year at college, she and about two or three hundred other kids were at a party at some house off campus. The cops showed up and, after they cleared everyone out, they found Annie hiding in the attic."

I smile. "It was a nice try. You have to give her that."

"Everyone called her Annie Frank for the rest of the semester."

I can't stifle my laughter. "That's terrible."

"I've lived through all the teenage stuff, Ally. Few parents, if any, are immune. As for me dealing with it again, your problems are mine now. That's the way marriage works."

I turn off the water and go to the vanity to twist up my hair. "We aren't married yet. There's still time for you to run."

"I'm not the one who's running. I don't need time." He pauses. "Do you want me to run?"

"You know I don't." Warren's never been one to lay on the pressure and guilt. But that's how this feels. Like he's backing me into a corner. "It's just...too much is happening to me right now. I can't even think about anything else but Nick and Sarah."

And Sonny.

I sigh and stare into the mirror at my sleep-deprived eyes. The wrinkles look deeper this morning. Lack of sleep, stress... and guilty feelings...will do it every time. Maybe Warren *wasn't* overreacting the other night. Maybe I am using Nick as a warped excuse to postpone facing what scares me most. Completely losing my heart and soul to another person and getting hurt because of it. Like I did with Sonny. With Sarah.

"I'm going to drive to Seattle this afternoon and meet with the Pachecos."

"Because?"

"Sarah gave them custody. She trusted them to raise him. So, maybe you're right about Randy. Maybe Nick just isn't used to having a man's discipline, so he went looking for someone he can intimidate and walk all over. Someone like me."

"You're tougher than that. Stand your ground with him. Quit being so afraid he won't like you."

"Easier said than done." I've learned that much in the past week. "Will you let him run around with you while I'm gone?"

"If you're sure that's what you want to do."

"I'm sure." Which isn't exactly true, but I'm at a loss as to what I *should* do.

"Why don't you come over here first while Nick helps out at the café for an hour or so. We need some time together."

"That sounds good."

"It will be." I hear the grin in his voice. "I promise."

After ending the call, I sink into the steaming water and close my eyes. I'll soak a half hour before calling Teena to ask her to handle things at the Pea for the second Saturday in a row. Then I'll call the Pachecos.

———

Nancy and Randy Pacheco are good, solid, hardworking people. He's a mechanic; she stays at home with their three kids, ages four, seven and eight. They don't have a lot, but they own their small three-bedroom house.

"He's not our problem." Randy reaches for the plate of chocolate cake his wife places on the side table next to his recliner.

Flushing scarlet, Nancy sits beside me on the sofa and scowls at him. *"Randy."*

"Pipe down, kids," Randy shouts, as the oldest of the three children chases the middle one through the living room, screeching. He turns back to us and takes a bite of cake. "I feel bad for the kid. I really do," he says between chews. "But, we got our hands full here as it is."

In the next room, a crash sounds, followed by giggling

shrieks. Randy's brows lift as he sets the plate aside and pushes out of his chair. "Like I said…"

When he leaves the room, Nancy looks down at her lap. "I'm sorry. Randy's blunt. That's just his way."

"Don't apologize. At least I know where he stands."

She looks across at me. "Sarah was my best friend for almost my whole life. I care about Nick. But I don't know him all that well. Not anymore. When he got older, he stopped letting people in."

"I understand."

"If our situation was different…" She glances around at the toy-strewn floor. "The truth is, we really don't have room for him. Nick was sharing a bedroom with the baby. I know that's hard for him. There's no place for his things. The kids go to bed early. He can't listen to his music at night or anything…" Her voice trails off. She bites her lower lip and averts her gaze from mine. "Nick's not easy. And I'm so busy raising my own kids, I'm afraid I can't give him the attention he needs…the discipline."

I don't mention that I have those same fears about myself.

"I know that, legally, he's mine and Randy's responsibility. But if you could—"

"I'll work something out," I interrupt, saving her from having to beg.

"Thank you." She blinks at me, her smile nervous. After an awkward moment, she widens her eyes and asks, "Would you like to see pictures of Sarah? We met in kindergarten so I have a lot of her."

My pulse kicks up at the prospect of seeing all the stages of my daughter's life. "I'd like that."

Nancy leaves the room, returning minutes later carrying

several photo albums and a carton of loose pictures. I find my reading glasses in my purse, slide them on.

As we turn page after page and shuffle through the snapshots that never made it into a book, my throat knots up until I can barely speak. Somehow, though, I manage not to cry while Nancy tells stories about herself and Sarah. I sense her struggling with her own emotions.

"This is our kindergarten dance recital." She hands me one of herself and Sarah dressed in tutus and tights before choosing another. "We must've been nine or ten here. It was a cold Halloween, I remember that."

I choke out a laugh. "What was she? A cucumber?"

Nancy's laugh echoes mine. "A pickle. And I was corn on the cob. Our friend, Carrie, was a—"

"Carrot?"

"You got it."

There's a shot of Sarah and Nancy wearing bikinis and sunglasses. Another of the two of them in prom finery and mums standing beside uncomfortable-looking young men in tuxedos. Then Sarah hugely pregnant, her smile not quite hiding the apprehension in her eyes.

All the years I missed. So much. A lifetime of love and laughter, problems and tears.

"Did Sarah ever talk to you about being adopted?" I ask.

Nancy closes the album in her lap. Turning her back to me, she returns it to the box on the floor at her feet. "Not really." She clears her throat. "I knew she was adopted, but we didn't talk about it much."

Her words say one thing, her body language, another. I want to ask more questions, encourage her to open up to me, but decide against it, suspecting she feels sharing hers and Sarah's private conversations would be a betrayal.

When I leave Seattle, I call Warren on my cell. He assures me things are okay. He says they spent the day hiking at Forest Park and not to worry about picking up Nick. Since I'll be in late, he can spend the night.

During the three-hour drive back to Portland, I have plenty of time to think about my visit with the Pachecos. About Nick and what's best for him. About Warren and me. But as the night passes by outside the car windows, my mind strays most often to the daughter I never met. According to Nick, she thought I owed her something. Do I? I never wanted to give her up. From the first moment I felt her move inside me, a tiny, fleeting flutter of butterfly wings against my stomach, I knew I wanted her with me forever. But my parents refused to help, financially or otherwise, if I kept her. So I told myself that the best thing I could do for her was to place her for adoption, like they insisted I do. She would have everything I couldn't provide. Both a mother *and* a father to love her. A grown-up, stable mother, instead of a confused teenage girl. A father who'd stick around. A real house with a yard to play in. Money for pretty clothes and toys.

During my visit, Nancy Pacheco confirmed that Sarah had those things I wanted for her. The Pearsons weren't rich, but they provided well enough for Sarah. They loved her, and she loved them. They were a family. They shared laughter, their problems, supported one another. Even when Sarah, at the age of eighteen and unmarried, announced she was pregnant, the Pearsons stood by her.

Unlike my own parents.

The car's headlights highlight the road stretching ahead into darkness. I do owe my daughter. That same support she had from her adoptive parents, the support I didn't have from mine. I owe it to her to see that her son is raised by the person most suited to provide him the love and guidance he needs. Someone with whom he can feel comfortable, safe and happy. If that person isn't me, I owe it to her to find out who is.

I see his face—the other person who owes Sarah. The missing part of our equation. He never had to deal with the consequences of his actions. He didn't have to make the tough decisions. He never ached over the loss of his child.

Sonny.

His green eyes haunt me while I drive. Smiling eyes, so young, so full of life and love. Gentle and patient, dancing with light. Wise beyond his years.

"What happened to you?" I whisper. "Why did you leave me?"

When I arrive home, I'm drained and exhausted but I know I won't sleep tonight.

I put on my pajamas and my reading glasses, fix a bowl of yogurt and fruit, carry it into my office. A box sits on the top shelf inside the closet. I drag a chair over and take it down. Mementos from the past are inside. Though I've tried, time after time, to throw them out, I have never brought myself to do it.

The tiny infant cap my baby wore in the hospital nursery fits in the palm of my hand. A kindhearted nurse brought it to me on the morning I went home. The Woodstock ticket I never used, since the fence around Yasgur's meadow had come down before we arrived, is creased and torn at one corner. A yellow glass-bead necklace Sonny gave me still shines in the lamplight. The daisy I wore in my hair is faded and dry beneath the cellophane I wrapped it in so long ago. At the bottom of the box, beneath old eight-track tapes of Carly Simon, Karen Carpenter and James Taylor, sits an envelope of pictures. I pick it up and slide the photos out.

On top is the image of a girl with straight dark hair to her elbows, parted in the middle. She wears a blue peasant blouse, the yellow bead necklace. The daisy from the box is in her hair, though in the photo, it's as bright and alive as her eyes.

I barely recognize myself. The girl smiling in the picture seems to be a totally separate person, someone vaguely familiar from a different life. Yet my heart remembers her hopes and dreams, her fearless strength and defiance, her lust for life.

I flip to the next picture and there stands Sonny, his arm around that dark-haired girl. My breath catches as I remember more of what she felt. A wild, all-consuming love for that lanky, scruffy, copper-haired boy. Love so powerful, I believed it would shield us from anything and everything the world tossed our way.

But I was wrong. So wrong.

Setting the photos aside, I go to the computer. It blinks to life when I turn it on, filling the dark room with an eerie blue glow. The screen saver is a photo of Warren and me at Multnomah Falls. I stand in front of him, his arms are draped around my waist. My hands cover his at my middle. His chin rests on my shoulder, and we're both grinning as the waterfall sprays mist behind us.

Only a month ago. And I was so unaware my life was about to change.

My love for Warren is gentler than what I felt for Sonny. Calmer. Grown-up love, not the reckless love of youth. Still, it's every bit as strong. But I'm not a naïve girl of sixteen anymore. I know that love can be ripped from my life in an instant if I'm not careful.

I move the mouse, click the icon for the Internet. When it comes up, I move the cursor to the Search box and poise my fingertips on the keyboard. I draw a breath, hold it, then type in "Sonny McGraw."

CHAPTER FIVE

"*How* ow do you know it's him?" Warren asks.

We stroll the river walk, side by side, not touching. No chance Nick will hear this conversation. He's far ahead of us on his new in-line skates.

I focus on the path but feel Warren's gaze. There's suspicion in it, hurt feelings, a trace of foreboding.

"There were two Mesquite Bend newspaper articles online that mentioned him as a resident. It's a little West Texas town. Apparently he farms and ranches there."

Warren clears his throat. "And the articles prove what? There could be more than one Sonny McGraw in the world."

"It has to be him. Sonny loved horses. We talked about him having a farm or a ranch some day." Or both.

I turn my head slightly, unable to stop the smile that curves my lips. I'd grow giant pumpkins and zucchini and...what else? Kumquats, yes. I draw my lower lip between my teeth as the warm memory of those silly dreams washes over me. *Allyson Cole's Colossal Kumquat Stand.* And green-eyed, red-haired babies. I'd grow those, too.

Does he have a dairy like Yasgur, the man who owned the Woodstock meadow? I doubt it. I don't know much about the Texas Panhandle, but I think it's known for cattle, not milk cows.

"Why don't you try to contact him first? You and Nick could go all the way to Texas and find out he doesn't even live there anymore."

"I called information, Warren. He's still listed." I step off the pathway, motion him over and place my hand on his arm. "Please don't ask me to explain, I'm not even sure why myself, but I want to look Sonny McGraw in the eye when I tell him we have a grandchild."

Warren's brows drew together. He purses his lips and stares off into the distance. "You wouldn't feel that way if you were over him."

"Over him?" I bark a laugh. "I was sixteen years old the last time I saw him. I'm fifty-two now, Warren. You think I'm not *over* him? A guy who's eighteen in my mind?"

He kicks a tuft of grass and watches me. "Honestly?"

I nod.

"No. I don't think you're over him. I think you've gone to sleep every night and woke up every morning for the past thirty-six years with his memory in the bed beside you. That's why you never fell in love with anyone else or married in all this time and why you've had such a difficult time admitting you loved me or agreeing to marry me."

Birdsong fills the spring air. My heartbeat picks up. Shaking my head, I step back. "That's crazy. I'm only curious about him. He left me. He disappeared without leaving a forwarding address or an explanation. I was angry at him."

"You're still angry. Because it's unresolved. The questions are still there and so are the feelings."

It's scary how well Warren knows me. I wouldn't admit there might be any truth to the possibility of me not being over Sonny until he spoke the words. I still can't really accept it. I couldn't be nursing feelings for my high-school lover after so many years; that's absurd. I'm a middle-aged woman. *Past* middle age.

Shielding my eyes from the sunlight with one hand, I turn away. Nicholas circles up ahead and begins his way back toward us.

Warren's right that I still wonder why Sonny left me. I never stopped wondering, not only about our baby, but about him. The questions and heartache, the betrayal, have stayed with me, tucked away in a hidden part of my heart for almost four decades. But that's no more than normal curiosity about an unsolved mystery in my life. The memories don't mean a thing.

"I have to do this for Nick, Warren. The boy is as much Sonny's as he is mine."

"His responsibility?"

Blinking, I turn back to him. "Yes, his responsibility. But not just that. Nick's his grandchild. Sonny has as much a right to know about him as me. He might be the best guardian for Nick. He might know how to handle kids. Maybe he's raised some of his own, who knows? We *won't* know unless I see him again."

"I think there's more going on with this trip than you delivering McGraw his grandson, Ally. Whether you want to admit it to yourself or not." Warren blows out a noisy breath. "I feel like I'm competing with the memory of your first love, and I hate it. I hate him. Do you know how ridiculous that makes me feel? How am I supposed to win?" His brows draw together. "Tell me how to compete with your past, and I'll do it."

"Warren…"

He heaves a sigh. "He's the father of your baby. A rose-colored memory. He'll always be young and wild and carefree. Then, there's me. I'm cold, harsh reality. A fifty-six-year-old man with graying hair and a bad back. On top of all that, I'm a bear in the mornings. How can I possibly compete?"

"Oh, Warren." A laugh chokes out of me, followed by a sob. "I love your grey hair. I love everything about you."

"I don't want you to go. But maybe you should. Maybe the only way you'll get over this is to see that the guy is none of those things you remember anymore." He shakes his head. "When you said you loved me and you'd marry me, I thought you'd finally let go of whatever it was you held on to. Then Nick showed up and you're back to where you were. Only now you're holding on tighter than ever."

Nick calls out to us as he streaks by.

My vision blurs as I look up at Warren. "Here." I pull off the ring he gave me and offer it to him. "Hold on to this for me, would you? I don't want to give it back, but I don't feel right wearing it with you feeling the way you do, either." I hold my breath, praying he won't accept it.

"My feelings aren't the ones that have changed, Ally." My heart sinks when he takes the ring and slips it into his pocket. "It's yours again when you're ready. All you have to do is ask."

A sound nearby brings my head around. Nick's no longer skating. He's stopped in the pathway, watching us. Our gazes lock, but I can't read him; maybe I never will.

"I'm sorry." Swiping at my eyes, I return my attention to Warren. "God, I'm so sorry. What's wrong with me? How have you put up with me this long?"

I don't know what I want anymore, but I'm sure it isn't this. Hurting Warren. Risking all we share.

He takes both my hands in his. "Will you fly?"

"I've decided to drive." I sniff. "To give Nick and me some time to get to know each other, like you keep telling me to do. I think we might even take the long way...go down the coast to L.A. From there, Nick might get a kick out of driving Route 66." The Mother Road. It seems appropriate. "And maybe with the two of us stuck in the car together for so many days, he'll be forced to talk to me. I'd like to learn more about Sarah, if nothing else."

He nods. "What about the café?"

"You were right. Teena, Joleen and Guy can handle it."

Warren's brow furrows, and I swear I hear his thoughts. *For Nick and Sonny McGraw, you'll allow it, but you wouldn't for me and our wedding.*

"When will you leave?" he asks.

"In a couple of days. I need to put some things in order first. I'll tell Nick tonight."

Nick steps off the path and begins taking off his skates, but he still watches Warren and me.

"He's going to be okay, Ally." Warren squeezes my fingers. "He has your strength."

I blurt a laugh and stare at the ground. "This is strong?"

He dips his head, forcing me to look at him. "You'll be okay, too." Warren nods toward Nick. "He loosened up some when we hiked yesterday. He told me some things about himself."

"Such as?"

"He used to play roller hockey. Which explains why he's such a pro on those skates. We had a good time together. He has your sense of humor when he forgets to act tough."

I remember Nick's ease with Beverly, with the customers at the café. Maybe it's only me he can't trust enough to warm up to.

And maybe I don't deserve his trust.

Or Warren's.

Two days later, I'm carrying my suitcases out to the car when Warren pulls up in front of the house. It's a cool morning and, according to the local weatherman, we'll have a mild, sunny day. Perfect for driving.

"Hello, Mr. Wesley," I call out to the elderly widower who lives next door. He pretends to water the bushes in front of his house, but water streams from the hose onto the walkway, since he's really watching me.

Warren joins me in the driveway where I set the bags down beside the Beamer. He hands me a stack of CDs and smiles. "For your trip down memory lane."

I flip through them. Janis Joplin. Crosby, Stills and Nash. Joe Cocker. "Where'd you get these?"

"When albums went by the wayside, I bought my old favorites on CD."

"That's quite a collection." I open the car door and put them inside. "Thanks."

"I'll want them back." He smiles, tucks a strand of my hair behind my ear when a breeze blows it into my face. "Soon."

I meet his gaze and smile, too. "Sure."

Warren clears his throat. "I'm sorry I've been scarce these past couple of days."

"It's okay. I understand."

He picks up the bags and follows me to the back of the car where he sets them down again. "Looks like you're all set."

"Now if I can just coax Nick out of his room, we'll be off."

"He doesn't want to go?"

"That's putting it mildly. He accused me of dumping him, like I did his mother."

"I'll talk to him."

"Don't waste your breath. You won't change his mind." I push the button on my key chain and pop the trunk. "I must be crazy making this into a road trip instead of flying. There'll be no escaping all his youthful angst and anger for the next several days."

"Talk to him about the Thunderbirds."

"The who?"

"Seattle's hockey team. He's a fan."

"You could fit what I know about hockey on the head of a pin."

He lifts his brows. "You want to get the kid talking, or not?"

Sighing, I ask, "What do I need to know?"

"For starters they're Western Hockey League. Seattle doesn't have NHL status."

"Whatever that is."

Warren laughs. "Just get Nick started. He'll fill you in." He lifts the suitcases into the trunk then turns to me again.

I straighten his collar, my throat closing at the intimacy of the gesture, though I've never given it a second thought the hundreds of times I've done it before. I have to go on this trip, I remind myself. It's important for Nick. *For me.* Maybe Sonny has the answers that elude me. About what's best for our grandson. *About how to move on with my life.*

Warren catches my gaze, holds it. "Before you go, I want you to have something else." Reaching into his coat pocket, Warren pulls out my engagement ring. It sparkles in the sunshine. "I never should've taken this back. It's yours, no matter what you decide."

Too emotional to speak, I reach up and cup his cheek with my palm then raise onto my tiptoes and press my mouth lightly to his. He smells like shaving cream. He smells like home. Like Warren. I'll miss him so much.

"You don't have to wear it if you don't want to, but I still want you to have it." His voice is quiet and heartbreaking.

I step back. Then, my eyes never leaving his, I hold out my left hand and spread my fingers wide.

Watching me, Warren slips the ring on.

At the sound of the front door closing, we both turn toward the house. Nick stands on the porch, his duffel bag over his shoulder, the suitcase I loaned him clutched in one hand. He stares at us a moment before starting down the steps.

"Hello, Nick." Warren pats the boy's back as Nick comes up beside us and loads his bags into the trunk.

"Hey."

"So, you're all ready to go?"

"No. She's making me."

"You'll have a good time." Warren closes the trunk. "Lots of great scenery along the way. You ever driven down the coast?"

"Nope."

"Well, you're in for a treat, then."

Nick jerks his head my direction. "That's what you said about her eggs and they weren't that great."

Warren's eyes narrow.

I lean against the back of the car and cross my arms. "Fire

away, Nick. You'll have to land a better shot than that to get under my skin. I'm used to snotty food critics."

For a silent minute that stretches on forever, I tap my foot and study my grandson. Then I push away from the car and head for the driver's side door. Opening it, I pause and look back at the two men in my life; one I know well, the other I'm beginning to think I'll never know at all.

They shake hands. "Goodbye, Nick," Warren says. "Don't give Allyson a hard time, you hear?"

"I'll be back for the float trip you promised. Don't forget."

"I won't."

"I'm not staying in Texas, no matter what she thinks. I'll hitchhike back on my own if I have to."

"I never said you'd have to stay," I call out, my frustration building. "I said we'll see what happens."

Leaning toward Nick, Warren lowers his voice. "Have an open mind. You never know, you might like it there."

"I'll be back."

After another gentle slap on the shoulder from Warren, Nick walks around to the passenger side of the Beamer and climbs in.

I'm about to climb in, too, when Warren meets me at my door. "Call me every night when you stop. I'll be worried about you."

I take his hand. "I'll call." Lifting onto my toes, I whisper in his ear, "I love you."

"I love you, too," he says quietly.

We embrace and, when he lets me go, I feel as if I've lost my anchor and I'm drifting off into unknown waters with an angry crew of one who wants to toss me overboard.

Pulling out of the driveway, we head to the end of the block and stop at the sign. I glance into my rearview mirror. Warren stands in the yard watching us.

I turn the corner.

We're over two hours into the trip and almost to the coast before I finally decide I've had enough of Nick's silent treatment. The MP3 player headphones haven't left his ears since we took off. From the corner of my eye, I see his head move ever so slightly to the beat of music I can't hear.

"You need to stop for anything?" My voice is raised, but he doesn't respond. Reaching across the seat, I tap his shoulder.

Nick jerks around to look at me, his eyes flashing, his face tight.

I point to my ear and he pulls the headphones off his.

"You need to stop for a bathroom break or a drink? Newport's twenty minutes ahead."

"I'm okay." He starts to put the headphones back on.

"Would you mind talking to me for a while? It's going to be a long, boring drive to Texas if we continue on like this the whole way."

"I've gotta have tunes."

"You want tunes?" I gesture toward the CD player where Harry Connick Jr.'s voice flows out, as smooth and warm as brandy. "You've got 'em."

Nick gives me a *yeah, right* look. "Not elevator *show* tunes."

"Okay." I smile and hit Eject, silencing Harry. "We'll give yours a try, then."

Hesitating, Nick turns and takes his backpack from the seat behind us. He digs through it, finds a CD, hands it to me.

Five minutes later, I hit Eject again. "Is that the sort of music you've been listening to since we left Portland?"

"Yeah."

"Don't you have a headache from all that screaming and screeching?"

His grunt clearly indicates I'm an out-of-touch, behind-the-times moron. A real old fogy.

"How about a compromise?" I lift one of the CDs Warren brought me, open the case with one hand and slide the disc in to play. "Janis Joplin," I say, as she yells, *All right! All right! I'm ready, man.*

Suddenly, I see her onstage in front of a mesmerized crowd, bleeding out her soul, as wild and unleashed and free as her frizzy long hair. I can almost taste the wine on my lips, swigged from a bottle when it passed my way. And I feel Sonny beside me, moving along to the music.

Nick mutters under his breath, keeping his gaze on the window. "That's not screaming and screeching?" he asks after a minute.

Good point.

Nick picks up the CD case and looks at the cover. "She scares me."

I scowl. "Janis?"

"Listen to her." He nods at the photo on the CD. "Look at her."

"How can you not like Janis?"

He shrugs and sets the case aside. "Didn't she die from a heroin overdose?"

I stop the music. "Something like that."

We drive another two miles in silence. Three. Four.

Nick crosses his arms. "I'll try not to make you mad anymore if we can go back."

He may look tough, but he sounds vulnerable. "This trip isn't about you making me mad, Nicholas," I tell him, feeling a stab of guilt. "It's about figuring out what's best for you."

"You think some old redneck in Texas is best for me?"

I smile at that description, remembering Sonny's long hair and offbeat clothes, his love of rock-and-roll music, the way he protested the war. "Sonny McGraw is far from a redneck."

"What's he like then?"

I open my mouth, take a breath, pause. "I don't know. Not anymore." Which stuns me. Up until Nick asked the question, I imagined we were headed toward an older version of the guy I remember. Kindhearted. Full of fun and big talk. Gentle. But, a puzzle, too. If he was all those things, why did he leave me in such a cruel way?

"You don't know what he's like? When was the last time you saw him?"

"It doesn't matter, I—"

"When was the last time?" Nick repeats, glaring at me.

I swallow. My heartbeat kicks up. "Thirty-six years ago."

"*Thirty*—you're gonna dump me with some guy you haven't seen for *thirty-six years*? A stranger? Have you even talked to him since then?"

The panic in his voice startles and shames me. "No, I…I was a stranger when you came to me, Nick."

"Mom checked you out. She read about your restaurant opening in a newspaper article online. She even drove to Portland and went there."

Disbelief punches me in the stomach so hard I grip the

steering wheel tighter to steady myself. "Your mother came to my café?"

He nods. "With Nancy."

Nancy Pacheco didn't tell me that. I remember her reluctance to reveal more than surface things about Sarah.

"They ate lunch and watched you work. Mom said you were nice to her. Nancy tried to get her to go to the counter and talk to you, but she ended up just asking for more bread."

For Nick's sake, I try to pretend I'm not shaking inside. "Why didn't she tell me who she was?" *Why didn't I recognize her?*

"She was afraid."

"Your mom told you that?"

"It's in her journal. I read it."

"Why was she afraid?"

Again, he turns to the window and the silence draws out between us. "Mom never would've asked me to find you if she knew you'd take me to some stranger. He could be a psycho—"

"He's not—" I stop myself. I'm nothing like the girl Sonny left behind. How can I be sure he's anything like the boy I remember?

"Mom thought you were a good person."

"Nick...calm down. Nothing's decided. I'm not dumping you with him. We're just going to meet him. He's your grandfather. He has as much right to know about you as I do. And you deserve a chance to meet him."

When we enter Newport, I pull into the first service station I see. Not because I need gasoline, because I need to calm my nerves.

In the restroom, I draw deep breaths and stare into the mirror.

Sarah came to the café. She watched me, talked to me. No

doubt, I looked at her hair, into her eyes, and wondered. Ached. Agonized.

My baby was within my reach, and I didn't even know it. She was close enough to hold in my arms again. We spoke to each other. But she was afraid.

Afraid of me.

Of my reaction.

When I return to the car, Nick's not there. I guess he must be inside the station. He might need money for a drink or a snack. I head in, and when I don't find him there, dread creeps up on me, an old nightmare that won't let me rest. I ask the attendant to check the men's room. It's empty, like I knew it would be.

I run outside, scan the road in every direction, calling Nick's name. Ignoring the stare of the man next to me filling his pickup, I check the Dodge Ram's bed and look into the cab, my anxiety stronger than the scent of gasoline fumes in the air.

The loud rumble of an engine starting brings my attention around to the pumps at the other side of the station. An eighteen-wheeler pulls out onto the road.

Waving my arms, I run toward it.

CHAPTER SIX

*N*ick sits in the passenger seat of the truck's cab, staring straight ahead at the road. Something tells me he sees me, that he knows I'm running alongside them.

I dart in front of the slow-moving truck and don't see the chug hole until it's too late. My foot falls in and my ankle twists. Pain shoots up my calf; a hot, searing knife slice. I cry out, but still manage to lift my arms and wave at the driver.

The truck's horn blares, and I squeal along with the brakes as the eighteen-wheeler comes to a stop ten feet in front of me. The driver's bald head appears outside the window. I can see that he's yelling, but I can't hear him over the idling engine's rumble.

When I don't budge, he pulls to the edge of the road, turns off the ignition and climbs out. "Lady, what the hell are you doing?" The man lumbering toward me is twice my size. He tugs up the waistband of jeans that ride below a belly as round as a watermelon. "I damn near didn't see you. I could've mowed you down."

Stooped over and panting, I rub my ankle.

"Are you okay?" He offers his arm.

I take it and stand, keeping the weight off my right foot. "I'm sorry, but you have my grandson."

He glances back at Nick. "That kid?"

"Yes."

Shaking his head, he mutters, "Little shit. Excuse my language, ma'am. The boy told me his car broke down and he needed a lift into Portland, which is where I'm headed."

With the man's help, I limp toward the truck. "We had a misunderstanding."

"I hear ya. I've got a few grandkids of my own." We stop alongside the passenger door. "You think you broke anything?"

I try my weight on the ankle again. "It's just a little sore. I'll be okay."

Nick doesn't move when the trucker motions him down, so the man opens the door of the cab himself. "Come on, son. Sounds like you've got a thing or two to work out with your grammaw."

Grandmother, I almost say, then feel my face heat up. It's silly to be so sensitive about the frail, frumpy images the other label conjures in my mind. I recall hearing my own mother tell my sister she didn't care what Bev's girls called her, as long as they called her. That's Mom's one example I wish I could be emotionally mature enough to follow. The only one. Why couldn't she have felt that way about *my* daughter?

Muttering under his breath, Nick climbs down while the trucker strokes my bruised ego by adding, "You don't look old enough to be this kid's grammaw, by the way."

"Thanks."

Minutes later, Nick and I sit in my car again. My hands

shake as I turn the key in the ignition. "Don't you ever pull a stunt like that again, Nick. What were you thinking?"

"I was going back."

"And where did you plan on staying when you got there?"

"With you."

"In case you haven't noticed, I'm here at the moment, not in Portland."

"You would've figured it out and followed me."

"Why do you want to stay with me, Nick? You act like you can't stand the sight of me."

He stares at his lap, blushes, his mouth twitching and his eyes narrowed to slits.

"You're not making it easy for me to learn to be a grandmother." I grip the steering wheel and blink at him. "This is new territory for me. Cut me some slack, okay?"

"Whatever."

"I told you, I'm not trying to get rid of you, if that's what you're thinking. But aren't you just a little bit curious about your grandfather? You might like him. Who knows? You might even like Texas. Which is why we're going there. To see. If you two hit it off and you decide you'd be happier staying there than with me, great. If not, that's fine, too. We'll go to plan B."

"I'm happy with you."

"I'd hate to see how you act when you're *unhappy*."

Tilting his head, he slants me an angry look, the old attitude resurfacing. "You bought me all that stuff and now I can't even use some of it. Like the computer. You sure wasted a lot of money."

So it's the computer we left behind that he likes. The things I can buy him, not me.

"I'll make sure you have your things, whether you're living with me or somewhere else."

A horn honks, and I realize I'm blocking the gasoline pumps. Wincing, I push my sore foot against the gas pedal, my nerves still teetering on a tight wire.

Nick stares at my trembling hand as I reach for the CD cases. "If your ankle hurts, I can drive."

"You have a license?"

His brows draw together. "I'm sixteen."

I send him a sidelong glance. "Frankly, I don't trust you not to pull another stunt if I let you behind the wheel."

"Whatever."

"Do you blame me, after what just happened?" I slide the CD into the player. "Like it or not, we're listening to Harry Connick Jr."

He grabs his MP3 player and headphones from the dash. *"You're* listening to him."

"That's right, I am."

Jamming the headphones on, he leans back and closes his eyes. "Fine."

Once again, I'm shut out. *Fine.*

The highway rises miles above the sea as we enter Florence, but the startling view is missed by Nick. His eyes remain closed, and I'm in no mood to make any suggestions I know will be shot down.

For the next fifty miles, sandy peaks loom within occasional gaps in the thick trees lining the road. I've been here before with Warren. A flower-lined trail at the state park leads to a towering sand hill overlooking a lake and a campground with a maze of dunes so tall, I felt as if I'd stepped onto the moon when we visited.

I consider pulling in at one of the access points to show Nick this amazing place. That's what I'd hoped to do on this trip. Explore with him, show him things he's never seen, have fun together and loosen us both up. But, as usual, Nick's unavailable to me, and after the incident with the trucker, I'm too emotionally weak to try to crack the wall of ice between us.

At the little town of Bandon, I do pull over. We eat on the waterfront then take off again, driving past stretches of wet, spongy ground where cranberries are grown, past patches of sheep-dotted meadows and Christmas tree farms.

In the rare moments when Nick's headphones are off, I comment about the blueness of the sky, the ocean, the lush green of the redwood forest as we pass the border into California. He nods or answers briefly, but makes no effort to carry on a conversation.

The sky darkens as we enter Mendocino, a pastel, pretty-as-a-postcard town set on a cliff, with crashing waves on one side and rugged woods on the other. I don't stop. When we left Portland, I thought I'd call it a day after no more than eight hours on the road, but since Nick seems content to snooze and listen to music, I continue on until we reach Gualala, an old logging port.

We check into a hotel, where I pay for a room with two beds. If they had handcuffs to lock Nick to the bedpost, I'd rent those, too. I'm too tired to keep an eye on him all night, and I doubt I'd hear him if he left the room. With stops along the way, we've been on the road more than twelve hours. I hope he's as tired as me and has no energy left to try anything, though I have my doubts about that.

Too wiped out to argue, I give in to Nick's suggestion and have a big, greasy pepperoni pizza delivered for him and a salad for me. After we eat, I put on my pajamas in the bathroom then fall into bed.

Stretched out on the bed beside mine, Nick watches television. I call Warren to let him know we're okay, check in with Teena, then pull the covers over my head. "You're not bothering me," I tell Nick, as if he asked. "Just keep the volume low, if you would."

During the night, I dream of Sarah. The five-year-old Sarah in the photograph Nancy Pacheco gave me, the little girl in a purple tutu and white tights. Pudgy and giggling, she dances to jewelry-box music. Copper curls fall from the clasp atop her head and bounce against her shoulders.

"Watch me, Mommy!" She rises up on her toes. *"I'm dancing. Help me twirl."*

I laugh and reach out to her, but she runs the opposite direction into the arms of another woman, the plump, smiling, pink-cheeked mother in the photograph.

"Sarah," I say, *"I'm your mommy."*

Turning in the woman's arms, Sarah's gaze meets mine, but there's no recognition in her eyes, only fear. Fear of a stranger. Me.

I wake up sobbing, the pillow damp beneath my cheek. Except for the glowing green 3:00 a.m. on the clock radio on the nightstand, the room is dark. For a minute, I don't remember where I am. When I do, I slip from the bed and make my way to the bathroom. I hear Nick's soft breathing, see the huddled shadow of his form on the bed beside mine.

The light hurts my eyes when I flip it on. In my purse on the vanity beside the sink, I locate the photos of Sarah in the inside zippered pocket. I take one out, put the lid down on the toilet and sit. Placing the photo on my knees, I prop elbows on my thighs and cover my mouth with my palms to muffle the sobs that rock me when I look at her face.

Sarah...Sarah. Why didn't you tell me who you were when you came to the café? I would've taken you in my arms, I would've told you how much I loved you.

The door squeaks. I look up.

Nick peeks in, his eyes sleepy and as soft as I've ever seen them. Soft and awkward and panicked. The sheepish look of every young man with a crying woman on his hands.

"The door was open," he mutters.

Pulling a strip of toilet paper from the roll, I wipe my face. "I guess the latch didn't catch. Sorry I woke you."

"Is your ankle okay?"

I'm seized by an overwhelming need to hug him, to comfort *him* more than myself. "My ankle's fine. I'll be out in a minute."

Before he shuts the door, his gaze drops to the photograph in my lap.

Minutes later, back in bed, staring up at the ceiling, silence bears down on me; I can barely breathe. I sense Nick is as wide-awake as me, that his heart, too, is swollen with words he can't squeeze out.

When I finally drift off, I sleep hard the rest of the night. Sweet, dreamless sleep. The kind I crave.

Midmorning, a finger of sunlight pokes between the drapes and nudges me awake. I yawn and stretch, surprised by how refreshed I am, considering my interrupted night.

Nick's bed is empty. The bathroom door is closed; a sliver of light shines beneath it. On the spare pillow beside me, I find a stack of four books held together with a thick, giant rubber band. They're all different sizes. The one on top is small and pink with daisies on the cover. The second one is larger, spiral bound, with a painting of a winding road on the front. The bottom two are thick, the covers, leather.

I jerk the rubber band off, lift the small book from the top, open the cover.

Centered on the first page in type are the words: JOURNAL OF, and on the line beside them in loopy script is scrawled the name *Sarah Pearson.*

"Nick?" I call out.

I get up, walk to the bathroom, knock on the door. No response.

My pulse chases me back into the room. While I throw on my clothes, scattered questions and fears collide in my mind. *What if I'm too late to catch him this time? What if he doesn't go back to Portland? What if I can't find him? And why? Why do I have to go through this again? Why do people leave me?*

Running to the door, I tug it open and almost bump face-first into Nick. I gasp and step back. Good thing the Styrofoam cup he holds has a lid on it or the contents would be on the floor.

He blinks wide eyes at me. "I was hungry. You were sleeping and I couldn't wait." He lifts the cup. "I brought you coffee."

It seems a peace offering. But I'm so relieved to see him, I can't say anything.

While Nick tosses yesterday's clothing into his duffel bag, I sit at the edge of the bed and sip the coffee, allowing my nerves to rearrange. "Nick?"

"Yeah?" He doesn't look up.

"Your mother's journals...are you sure you're okay with me reading them?"

He zips the bag, puts it on his bed then places his MP3 player on top of it. "Yeah."

"Because if you're not—"

"I said I'm sure." Picking up the TV remote, he pushes a button. Voices fill the room.

"Thank you, Nick."

He shrugs, his eyes on the screen.

I put down the coffee cup and go to the bathroom to clean up. The drive to the next hotel will be a long one. Longer than yesterday's drive, no matter where we finally stop.

Until then, I won't have time alone to read, to savor every word, consider every thought. To meet my daughter for the very first time.

CHAPTER SEVEN

September 14, 1988

Dear Diary,

Sarah here. I feel dumb writing to someone who doesn't exist. I mean, who am I really talking to? Myself, I guess, since Ms. Rodale says these journals are private, that she won't read them or anyone else. That's my senior English teacher's name— Ms. Rodale. *Ms.*, not Miss or Mrs. She's sort of a flake. She cries while reading "Death Be Not Proud" aloud. I like her, though. I mean, really, that book makes me want to cry, too. Besides, her funky clothes are cool and she plays classical music for us. Starting today, we "journal" the first ten minutes of class to "get in touch with our inner voice." Heavy stuff, as Ms. Rodale would say. I bought this diary because of the daisies—my favorite flower.

What else? Gary. He is SO HOT! I can't stop thinking about him. He hasn't called once since we did it last month at Carrie's party. I guess he got all he wanted from me and he's moved on to Karen Potter. I wish I hadn't drank that night. Maybe I would've been strong enough to say no to him. Or maybe not. One thing is for sure—I'm *not* driving by his house again.

Ms. Rodale is telling us to finish up. More later.

While Nick returns to the hotel room for the toothbrush he forgot, I sit in the car and read Sarah's first journal entry. Closing the cover, I stare at the daisies. Her favorite flower. She would've been eighteen in September of 1988.

I want to tell her to forget about Gary. That any guy who would have sex with her then ignore her because he got what he wanted is bad news.

Then, I do some arithmetic and realize Gary might be Nick's father. If there'd been no Gary, would there be no Nick?

Life never ceases to confuse me. Maybe things we do that seem like mistakes are really meant to be. Or maybe it's all haphazard, no rhyme or reason. Good can bloom out of a bad situation, heartache from happiness.

When Nick comes out, I start the ignition. Though it's cloudy, he wears sunglasses.

"Your eyes bothering you?" I ask when he climbs in beside me. He seems to use a lot of eyedrops.

"Allergies."

"Spring pollen gets to you, huh? Mine start in the summer."

Things are less tense between us today. As we head for San Francisco, he leaves the headphones off. I talk. To myself, it seems. Long stretches of time go by when he doesn't comment at all, not even a word, and I get the feeling he's tuned me out.

Still, I consider the loss of the headphones progress. One baby step at a time. That's all I ask.

The highway clings to the shoreline through pines and redwoods, past rocky coves and crashing blue Pacific waves. Air, salty clean and sharp, rushes in through my open window.

I glance across at Nick. "Why don't we spend some time in San Francisco?"

"Okay."

"Warren's always trying to get me to go there with him for a vacation. That's where he grew up. I think he wants to show off his old haunts."

"You won't go?"

"We spent a day and a night there last summer. I checked out some of the popular cafes around the city." I smile across at Nick, happy that we're actually having some semblance of a real conversation. "It's always good for business to stay tuned in to the competition. Have to keep evolving, you know? But I couldn't stay more than one night, like Warren would've liked. Had to get back to the Pea."

"He said you're a workaholic."

Ouch. "He did?"

Nick nods. "At the store the other day. He told some guy he ran into he didn't know if he could drag you away from the café for a long honeymoon 'cause you're such a workaholic."

I squint ahead at the road. I don't think of myself in that way and didn't know Warren did, either. Is that what I've become? A workaholic? So caught up in my career I have trouble relaxing or taking a vacation? Is bed the only place I allow myself to let loose? Warren's never complained about that.

Whatever happened to the girl with the flower in her hair, the yellow beads and blue peasant blouse? She lived for the moment, gobbled up life like a big bowl of ice cream, unconcerned about her face getting messy or her fingers sticky.

I know the answer to that. Her recklessness led to loneliness and questions. A baby she couldn't keep. To an obsession with achieving dreams and proving to the people who'd failed her that they weren't needed. Not Sonny. Not her parents. Not anyone. She could make it alone.

That girl turned into me. The workaholic.

I'm still stewing over my fiancé's image of me as an all-work-no-play, or at least mostly-work-little-play, kind of girl when Nick and I stop at the Muir Woods National Monument to see the giant redwoods. Later, I'm as quiet as him when we cross the Golden Gate Bridge into the city.

Despite the mistakes I made in my youth, I realize I miss that girl from long ago. I miss my old spontaneity, the ability I had to make the best of a bad situation, to lift my arms skyward and welcome the rain, when what I'd really hoped for was sunshine. My failed trust in Sonny stole all that from me; I changed the day he left, said goodbye to that girl and her idealism and never looked for her again.

Nick and I walk around Fisherman's Wharf then watch the fat sea lions sunning themselves off the pier. One wakes up frisky and nudges his sleeping neighbor into the water. They bellow and complain to one another, and Nick throws back his head and laughs. A deep, joyful belly laugh that lifts my soul and stirs more memories. It's the first time I've heard him laugh so loud, yet the sound is familiar. As familiar as his eyes.

Later, we sit on bar stools at an outdoor waterfront café eating a late lunch. Seagulls peck at dropped crumbs on the pavement around us. The air smells of salt and fish and sunshine. Nick is between me and a toothless old man wearing a beret, who strikes up a conversation with him.

"Sixteen, are you? What'll you be? A junior in high school next year?" The old man gums a French fry.

"A sophomore."

"Ah…a sophomore. Sixteen." He clicks his tongue. "The best years of your life. Don't let it pass you by. Store up the memories. What's your best one so far?"

It's as if they've forgotten I'm here, allowing me the freedom to lean back, watch and listen. To study my grandson without him noticing and shutting down.

"My best memory so far about high school?" Nick asks.

"The one thing you'll remember and cackle over when you're an old man like me. The one everybody at your fiftieth reunion will still be talking about."

Nick takes another bite of sandwich. I see him in profile, his face fixed in concentration. One foot taps against the railing below. After a minute, he swallows and smiles. "My best high-school memory so far is the bet I had last year with my friend Elliott to see who could go all year without wearing underwear." He and the man both laugh.

After finishing off his sandwich, Nick says, "But the best memory of all time was in middle school. Eighth grade. Me and Elliott found a way into the ceiling over the cafeteria. We crawled up there looking for a crack or a hole we could look through. But then the ceiling tiles caved in under us and we both fell through."

Shrieking, the old man pulls off his beret and slaps it against the bar top. "Were kids in there eating at the time?"

Nick snickers and nods. "I landed on the floor, but Elliott

landed on Lacy Macintosh's tray, right in front of her on a table. He smashed her hamburger."

The old guy hoots, and I bite back my own laugh. "So what happened?" he asks.

"We got suspended for a week, and Mom grounded me for three."

"Was it worth it?"

"Yeah." Nick laughs. "It was. The day they let us back in school, all the guys treated Elliott and me like rock stars." He gets quiet for a moment then adds, "My mom, she ragged on me about it, but she had trouble not laughing, too. Finally, she just lost it. Both of us did."

He shifts a bit on the stool, glances at me then returns his focus to the man. "She was like that. She knew what to really get upset about and what to just warn me about and then let it go. I mean, it's not like Elliott and me hurt anybody except ourselves."

"My mama still would've paddled me black and blue," the old man says.

"What about you?" Nick asks him. "What's your favorite school memory?"

The old man doesn't hesitate. "Lightin' blue blazers in the football locker room."

Frowning, Nick takes a drink of his Coke. "Blue blazers?"

"Farts."

Coke spews out Nick's nose; I almost choke on my drink.

"I don't recommend it," the old man adds. "Singed the hair right off my ass."

We spend another hour in San Francisco then continue south down the coast. Nick offers to drive and, though I'm hesitant, I let him. He's given an inch with me by sharing Sarah's journals. I take it as a sign of growing trust. I suppose it's my turn now.

Soon, I'm yawning. I guess Nick talked himself out with the old man on the waterfront, because he's quiet again. The lack of conversation, the hum of the car and my middle-of-the-night crying jag catch up with me and lull me to sleep.

I don't know how much time passes while I'm out, but when I awake, the car is stopped on the side of a small road shadowed by overgrown sycamore trees, it's pouring rain, and Nick is nowhere in sight.

Thinking he must've needed a quick bathroom break in the trees, I wait. When five minutes pass and he's still not back, I roll down the window and yell his name. He still doesn't show, so I get out. I should've known he'd run away again given half a chance.

The short trail I follow becomes muddier by the second. It leads through a grove of trees and eventually opens onto a sprawling white sand beach. Between where I stand and the shore, two huge rocks at least nine or ten feet tall sit side by side. One has a slight overhang, and through the heavy downpour, I recognize the form of a person standing beneath it.

"Nick!" The tree I'm under is poor shelter from the rain. I cup my hands around my mouth and try again. "Nick!"

I squint, see him lift his hand to his face. He's smoking. Sneaking cigarettes again. I take off across the beach toward him, cursing the rain with each soggy step, cursing Nick and my own stupidity for letting him drive then falling asleep.

The second he sees me, he drops the cigarette and starts

toward me. When we catch up to each other, I grab his arm and tug him back toward the trail.

"Hey!" Nick half grins, half scowls as he tries to twist his arm from my grasp. "Come look at these tide pools. They're awesome."

I continue walking and don't let go.

"I'm coming. You don't have to drag me."

"Why do you keep doing this to me?" I yell.

"Doing what?"

"Disappearing. Scaring me to death. Are you so addicted to cigarettes you had to pull over and smoke one?"

"Don't freak out. It's no big deal."

By the time I reach the trail, my hair is plastered to the back of my neck and my clothes cling to my skin. I'm furious. Fuming. I'm surprised steam doesn't rise from my drenched body. Tugging Nick's wrist behind me, I step into the trees. My foot, the one with the sore ankle, comes down on a slick, wet rock and goes out from under me. Nick and I both fall. I land on my butt in the mud, the breath jarred from my lungs, with Nick down beside me.

"*Shit*," I cry out. Though I'm not really hurt, tears scald the backs of my eyelids.

Nick blurts a laugh. The sound is so unexpected, my heart jumps. I shove his shoulder. "It's not funny. If you'd stayed on the highway like you were supposed to…" Planting both hands in the mud, I push to my feet, but the soles of my flip-flop sandals are slick. In seconds, I fall on my butt again.

Hot tears, as unstoppable and annoying as the rain, seep from my eyes. For several seconds the only sound is my quiet sobbing, the ocean waves and the patter of raindrops on the umbrella of leaves above.

Nick's laughter begins again. Shaking with anger, I glare at him.

His hand covers his mouth and, when he drops it, his cheeks are smudged with mud. "I'm sorry." He straightens his face, but only for a second. "I'm sorry." He snickers.

I flash back to another mud-smeared face with the same narrow, smiling eyes. But the hair is copper and much longer than Nick's.

"I'm sorry, Al. It's just...you look so funny."

"You're sorry?" I grinned. "I'll show you sorry." Balling my muddy fist, I flicked my fingers, splattering him worse.

He splattered me back.

Squealing, I grabbed a handful of mud and threw it. Then we were smearing each other's faces, laughing and yelling, slipping and sliding in the muck.

I blink away the memory until it's Nick I see before me again. Lifting my hand, I smear it down his face.

His startled expression makes me grin. Seconds pass in silence before we both start laughing. And it feels good, so good to let go of the tension, like I haven't laughed in years. For once, I allow myself to savor a large, sweet dose of joy without adding a pinch of guilt to dull the taste.

Nick finally pushes to his feet and offers me his hand.

Still giggling, I reach up. "You promise you're not going to let me go?"

He tugs. "I promise."

We're standing face-to-face when I catch a whiff of his breath. The sweet, smoky scent is one I haven't smelled in years. I look at Nick, really look, and my heart sinks. I know that slow-motion, red-eyed haziness. I experienced it many times in another life. I don't want to overreact, but now that the tables are turned, I don't know how to handle the situation.

We rinse the mud off in the icy-cold ocean. Once we're back in the car and on the road again, me driving this time, I don't confront Nick about what I smelled on his breath. It explains a lot of things that I had hoped were signs he was becoming more comfortable around me. The fact he was only mildly annoyed when I dragged him toward the trail, his easy, fitful laughter. Instead they were signs of something else.

My grandson is stoned.

I'm conflicted. And ashamed that I am. I smoked a lot of pot at Nick's age and thought nothing of it. Sometimes I thought that the world would be a better, more peaceful place if everyone stayed high. At Woodstock, five hundred thousand kids, most of them stoned, existed together peacefully in what was later deemed a disaster area. Not enough food or water, bathroom facilities or dry shelter. Still, other than the use of illegal drugs, the participants committed no crimes at the site or in the surrounding towns. No thefts, no rapes, no murder. Other than one reported punch to the nose, no one even got beaten up. Everyone shared what they had and helped one another. Even the older residents of the area remarked on the politeness of the young people.

Despite all that, I have hindsight on my side now. I'm realistic enough to know that too much herb-induced happiness and cooperation often comes at a cost.

At the first gas station, we pull in and change into dry clothes. Every second I'm away from Nick, I worry he'll be gone when I exit the restroom. But when I return to the car, I find him sitting inside, barefoot, humming and eating a big bag of barbecue potato chips.

I slide behind the wheel and slam the door. "Those are really bad for you."

"And they taste really good. Mmm." He holds out the bag to me. "Want one?"

Ignoring him, I start the car.

Nick dozes off and stays out most of the rest of the way to our next stop for the night in a California farming town called Cambria, where Hearst Castle stands.

I decide to wait until dinner before bringing up the marijuana. The mellowing effects of his high have worn off and I hope that, surrounded by people, he'll be less likely to make a scene.

Just off Main Street, I find a restaurant that serves vegetarian food. Nick could use a healthy meal after all the munchies he consumed in the car today.

He frowns at the menu. "Don't you have anything regular?" he asks the waitress, whose short, blond hair is woven into hundreds of tiny spiked braids.

"If by 'regular' you mean decaying animal flesh, you came to the wrong place."

"Anything with cheese?"

She blinks at him from behind her tiny, black, rectangular glasses. "We have a spinach salad with feta cheese and portobello mushrooms."

"That sounds good," I say. "I'll have that."

Nick makes a face. "What I really want is a hamburger with American cheese."

She settles a fist on one hip. "The best I can do is a tofu burger with alfalfa sprouts."

"Okay, that's what I want," Nick says, then grumbles, "I guess."

"Your arteries will thank you." She lifts her chin. "So will the cows."

"And a Coke," Nick adds.

I tap my foot against the floor as the waitress launches into a diatribe about killing poor, defenseless animals, and Nick pummels me with dirty looks.

When she finally leaves, he lifts his fork and knife and drums the tabletop.

I sit back. "So...how long have you been smoking dope?"

The drumming ceases. He blinks. "Huh?"

"You were smoking a joint on the beach this afternoon."

"That was a regular cigarette. You said so yourself."

I tear the wrapper off a cracker. "That was before I smelled your breath."

His lip curls. "How would you know what weed smells like?"

I bite into the cracker and chew slowly to buy time. Okay, what now? Be truthful? Hedge? Lie? Middle ground feels safest. "I was a teenager in the sixties, Nick. I've smelled my share of pot."

He stretches one arm across the back of the booth, his eyes locking with mine. "Did you smoke it?"

"I—yes." Maybe it's best that he knows *I* know what I'm talking about.

"Let me guess. You didn't inhale."

Somehow, I manage not to flinch at his sarcasm. "I inhaled plenty."

His brows lift, and I get the distinct feeling he's seeing me for the very first time. "So, what? Now you're going to give me the do-as-I-say-not-as-I-did speech? Before he died, my grandpa used that one on me all the time."

I hold up a hand. "No speeches. I just think we should

discuss this. I want to point out some things for you to think about. First of all—"

"Did you *like* getting high?"

My breath catches. "Whether or not I liked it isn't the issue. It's a foolish, risky habit. A waste of time if you do it too much. That's what matters."

"That's what I thought. You liked it."

"Here you go!" The waitress shows up with our drinks.

Nick stops her. "I was wondering…do you have brownies for dessert?"

"Why, yes, we do. Sugar free, of course."

"Plain or special? My grandma really likes the *special* kind." He wiggles his brows.

The waitress's eyes widen, and she giggles. Then, pulling herself together quickly, she looks at me. "Um…sorry. Ours are just plain." She backs away.

My face burns. Leaning across the table toward Nick, I lower my voice. "When we get back to the room, I want your stash."

He grins. "No problem. I'll share."

"I want it all."

"Wow, you *do* like it."

"Funny, Nick. For your information, I'm going to get rid of it. If we're stopped and the police find it in the car, I could go to jail."

He pushes his drink away. "What makes you think I have anymore?"

My head pounds along with my heart and, for the first time in my life, I feel guilty for all the hell I put my parents through when I was a kid. "We can make this easy or hard, Nick, it's up to you. If you aren't willing to give it to me, I'll search your bags and all your pockets and anywhere else I can think of until I find it."

His face darkens. "So it was okay for you, but not for me."

"Like I said, I was foolish. And lucky I didn't get in trouble with the law."

He barks a laugh. "I guess next you're going to give me that 'it leads to harder drugs' bullshit."

"Don't put words in my mouth. But it does lower your inhibitions about trying harder stuff. And, like it or not, it's against the law. What if you get caught? A police record can affect your college prospects. Finding a job. It just isn't worth it."

"You're a little late warning me about that."

I take a drink of hot tea, then set the cup down as the implication of his statement hits me. "What are you trying to tell me?"

All his smugness evaporates. His tongue flicks across his upper lip as he averts his gaze to the tabletop. "Nothing. It's no big deal. Don't worry about it."

"You hinted at something, now say it."

"My mom was always worrying about me and look where it got her. He turns away. "I told her I was okay, but she wouldn't stop."

"Nick...I'm sure her worrying about you had nothing to do..." I reach across the table and touch his arm. "It didn't cause her to get sick."

He slaps my hand away, startling me. "You don't know anything. The doctors said stress could make her worse. If not for me—"

"Here you go..." The waitress delivers his tofu burger and my salad, interrupting us again.

Nick pushes out of the booth and leaves his food, and me, behind.

After the waitress puts our meals in to-go cartons, I find Nick back in the motel room. While he watches television, I step into the hallway and call Nancy Pacheco on my cell. When pressed, she tells me that, last year, Nick got slapped with a minor-in-possession-of-alcohol charge, then, a couple of weeks later, a charge for possession of marijuana.

He straightened up when he saw how upset his mother became. Sarah was already in chemo by then, and Nick was having a hard time dealing with her illness. He started making his curfew on time, began helping out more around the house. No more incidents occurred with alcohol or drugs.

Then Sarah died, and the problems immediately started again. Only, this time, they seemed indicative of more than a reckless kid having too much fun.

When I ask Nancy why she didn't tell me all this before, she claims not to have thought of it, but I suspect she was afraid I'd scare off and leave her to handle Nick's problems alone.

After I end the call and return to the room, Nick gives me a joint that he pulls from the pocket of a folded pair of jeans. "That's all of it?"

He nods.

"You're sure? Like I said, if we're caught with this in the car, I could get in trouble, too."

"I said, that's it."

"Okay. I trust you."

His eyes meet mine briefly then return to the television.

A call to Teena brings me a measure of relief when she assures me things are running smoothly at the Pea. Relief, and a little disappointment. For years, I've convinced myself the place wouldn't survive more than a day without me, but that doesn't seem to be the case.

After talking to Teena, I call Warren.

"I thought about you all day," he tells me. "I know you're having a tough time. I wish I could be more help."

"It's okay, honey. I'm fine."

The warmth of his voice makes me wonder, again, what's wrong with me? What am I doing out here on the road, instead of home with him where I belong? Why didn't I just call Sonny, tell him about Nick and take care of all this over the phone? Nick could've flown to Texas alone. There's no reason for me to see Sonny. It doesn't matter why he left me. It happened eons ago and doesn't affect me now, one way or the other. At least that's what I try to convince myself.

Despite Nick's earlier assurances, I can't sleep. Around 2:00 a.m., when his steady breathing assures me he's out, I take his bags into the bathroom and search them. Hidden between the torn lining of his duffel are two more rolled joints, a baggie of weed and rolling papers.

I start to dump it all down the toilet then stop myself. I could get rid of it, flush it all away. But I can't get rid of his problems, his guilt and grief, that easily.

I tuck everything back where I found it, knowing it's a risk, but suddenly willing to take it. Nick deserves another chance to do the right thing. I said I trusted him. This is my chance to prove I mean it.

CHAPTER 8

March 3, 1989

Dear Diary,

The sonogram says it's a boy. Knowing that makes this little person growing inside me all the more real. Just like the first time he moved did. Mother and Daddy are still trying to talk me into giving him up, but there's no way I'll do it. They keep throwing in my face the good life they've given me, the nice home, their affection. That's all true, and I love them, but they don't understand. I don't want my son lying in bed at night wondering, like I did. If his hair is red, I want him to know that it came from me. If his eyes are blue, it's because Gary's are, too. Most of all, I don't want him hurting inside, thinking—why didn't she love me enough to keep me? What was more important? Doesn't she worry? Does she think about me at all?

Now that I know how it feels to have a child moving inside me, how my love grows with it until it's bigger than anything—my belly, my fears, the world—I wonder all the more about my real mom. How could she let me go? Give me to strangers? Was her heart so different than mine?

I don't care if Gary left. I don't care if my parents decide not to help me. I don't care what happens. I will take care of my baby. Nothing will stop me. Nothing else matters. ~Sarah

---

Almost six hours have passed since we stopped in L.A. for lunch then saw a few sites, and I'm desperate for conversation. Nick's earphones are finally off so I'm taking full advantage of it. I'm tired of talk radio and my own thoughts. No matter what I do to try to stop them, they inevitably drift to Sarah lying in bed as a little girl, wondering about me, thinking I didn't love her. That I traded her for something I considered more important.

My daughter was braver than I was. Stronger.

And older, I remind myself. I was only seventeen when she was born, while she was nineteen when she had Nick. But should two years make any difference? No matter how young I was, it doesn't change the fact that I was a mother with a mother's emotions.

"We'll stop at the Grand Canyon tomorrow."

"Okay," Nick says, sounding unenthused.

"You want to, don't you?"

"I don't care. If you do."

He doesn't care. I tap the steering wheel. Recalling Warren's advice, I say, "Tell me about your hockey team."

Nick shoots me a frown. "What do you want to know?"

"Tell me about your last game."

"You watch hockey?"

"Some." When he doesn't offer any information, I ask, "Do you like playing?"

"If I didn't I wouldn't do it."

Strike one.

"You think you'll keep it up?"

"That depends. Do they have hockey arenas in Texas, or do they just slap cow patties around a field with a great big tree limb?"

Strike two.

"Who's your favorite team?"

"The Ducks." He slides a sarcastic look my way. "Who's yours?"

I search my memory for the Seattle team Warren mentioned. "The Thunderbirds."

Nick appears surprised, but his expression quickly changes to suspicion. "Your favorite NHL team."

Well, damn. "The Redskins?"

He mumbles under his breath and says, "The Redskins are a football team."

Strike three. I wince. "Oh."

Time for a new topic of conversation. One I'm better versed in. "It's getting late. You want to stop for the night in Kingman? It isn't far. I hear they have a great diner along old Route 66 there. I've read about it. We could try it for dinner."

"A diner? You mean we actually get to eat something normal tonight? Good. I could use a junk-food fix."

"You've had plenty of unhealthy food on this trip."

"Not as much as I'd like."

"You've developed some very bad habits."

"And you've developed some fanatical ones. What got you so into cooking and stuff, anyway?"

A question about me. Finally. Another baby step. "It was the one thing I enjoyed doing with my mom. She taught me a lot."

"Why health food?"

"I'm not sure. Maybe to aggravate her. To rebel." That sudden realization surprises me. "She cooks with lots of butter and bacon fat and salt. It's the only way, in her opinion."

"Mine, too. Your mom sounds great."

"She was."

"She's dead?"

"No."

"So, she's not great anymore?"

"I'm sure she is. At cooking, anyway." I feel his gaze. "My parents and I have a few issues."

From the corner of my eye, I see his brows bob. "Have you always had your own café?"

"Up until ten years ago I was a chef in other people's restaurants to learn the ropes. My father thought it was beneath me. Once, when he didn't know I was listening, I heard him refer to me as nothing more than a short order-cook. Even though these were high-class places, and I was making a name for myself."

He tilts his head. "So, you opened the Slender Pea to prove something to them?"

This kid has X-ray vision; he sees too much. "Maybe so."

Maybe so.

All the small Arizona towns we've passed through are starting to look alike. The one we pull into just after sunset is no exception. We arrive in silence. That is, until Nick spots a small traveling carnival set up in a parking lot just off the interstate.

He sits straighter. "Pull over."

For reasons I can't explain, the twinkling array of colored lights makes me nervous. "Why? You showed zero interest in the Muir Woods when we stopped there and you're not that excited about the Grand Canyon, but you want to see this? You can go to a carnival any time. They're a dime a dozen."

"I like them." When he sees the frustration on my face he adds, "I'm bored."

Groaning, I turn into the lot.

Music plays from the rides along the midway. Carnies shout and children squeal. The scent of over-buttered popcorn and burned sugar drifts on the air. They're the same sounds and smells from the carnivals of my youth; that hasn't changed. A long line stretches to the pay booth at the entrance. A sign says six dollars to get in, or fifteen for a hand stamp honoring all the rides.

"That's a rip-off," Nick says, his voice low. "We're not gonna be here long enough to pay that much. Come on."

Relieved that he has come to his senses, I follow him, my sandals slapping the soles of my feet. But at the edge of the fence, he turns down a dark alley that runs behind the carnival booths instead of heading the opposite direction to the car.

The backyards of houses line one side of the alley, the backs of the carnival booths line the other side. Most of the house windows glow orange and gold with light. Back doors stand open to welcome the warm May breeze in. "Where are you going?" I glance over my shoulder, my nerves on full alert.

"To the free entrance."

"Free—" I jog a few steps to catch up, my sore ankle aching and wobbling on the rocky, dirt surface of the alley. "There's no free entrance."

"Sure there is. Every carnival has one. You just have to find it."

We pass a man in an undershirt emptying his trash into a Dumpster. "Hello, sir," I say. He stares, then heads back for the house, dragging the can and mumbling.

"Nick, stop," I hiss. "We can't do this. We'll get in trouble. Come back to the car right this minute, do you hear me?" Apparently not. He walks so fast I can't stay in step with him. "I'm not wearing the right shoes. We could get mugged."

Nick glances back at me. "If you want to pay, go ahead. I'll meet you at the Ferris wheel."

"I'll pay for both of us. It's not that much. I don't mind."

He keeps moving. We reach the end of the carnival grounds. The booths here are quieter. They might even be empty, but since we're at the back of them, I can't be sure. A television blares in the house across the way.

Nick grabs hold of the chain-link fence while dread grabs hold of me. And squeezes. A dog growls in the yard of the house with the loud TV. "Come on." Nick rattles the fence. "You first. I'll help you over."

"Young man..." I feel like I've morphed into my mother again. "We are not going over that fence. Do you understand me? I *forbid* you to go over it." Well, wonderful. Now I not only sound like my mother, I sound like my father, too.

Standing on one foot, I dig a pebble out of the sole of my opposite sandal. Behind me, the dog's growl seems closer, more menacing. I'm so furious with Nick, my mind only half registers the sound.

"It's okay." Nick reaches out a hand to me. "I've done this lots of times. It'll be fun."

"This is insane. It's wrong." I slip the sandal on again. "I can pay the entry fee."

"And waste a good twelve bucks?"

The dog barks. Turning, I realize no fence encloses the yard. In the middle of it, two glowing red eyes pierce the darkness.

"Tor!" A woman's voice calls from the back door of the house. "Come in now. Don't you go out in that alley, boy, ya hear?"

Nick lets go of the fence. "Don't move," he says quietly. Inching toward me, he takes my hand then breathes, "Run!"

We take off.

Blood rushes in my ears, muffling the sounds of barking, the woman's shouts, our feet pounding the dirt alley. We kick up dust. The purse slung over my shoulder beats against my hip.

When I start to glance back, Nick yells, "Don't look!"

I see the car ahead, let go of his hand and start fumbling to get the keys from my purse. Five steps from the car, I finally grab hold of the chain. I hit the button to unlock the doors. Nick's already around to his side. We swing both doors open at the same instant, fall inside, slam them.

Seconds later, the snarling face of a pit bull appears at my window.

"Ohmygod! Ohmygod! Ohmygod!" I grab my throat and press back into the seat.

Nick doesn't make a sound until a disheveled, panting woman in curlers and a bathrobe appears behind the dog. Startled, he shrieks and she shrieks back, her eyes bugging out. Then she grabs the dog's collar and yells, "Tor, you son of a bitch."

We both explode, Nick and I. I press my palms to my aching chest, unable to stop the laughter pouring out of me, barely able to breathe. Tears stream down my face. Beside me, Nick hangs his head between his knees, gasps for air and laughs, too.

For a while, I close my eyes, lean back against the seat, suck in air. When I finally calm down, I look across at Nick. "I don't think I've ever felt so terrified." *Or so alive.* At least, not in a very long time.

Lifting his head, he glances over at me and grins. "Sorry about that."

A hundred reprimands come to mind, but I can't bring myself to utter even one of them. "What was that all about, anyway?"

"You really want to know?"

"I really want to know."

"I needed a cigarette."

"All that for a cigarette? I don't get it."

"I knew you wouldn't buy me a pack, and I don't have enough money left to buy one myself. But I do have enough to play the bottle toss. And I'm good at it. All the carnies smoke. I figured when I won, I'd ask if I could trade my stuffed animal prize for a couple of smokes."

"That must be some powerful nicotine fit you're having to come up with that scheme."

"You can't expect me to quit just like that." He snaps his fingers. "I've been smoking since I was, like, thirteen or something."

"Why wouldn't you just let me pay our way in?"

"And spend twelve bucks for two cigarettes?"

Crossing my arms, I study him. I started smoking after Sarah was born. Ten years later, I quit after deciding it wasn't the right image for a chef specializing in healthy gourmet. Giving cigarettes up wasn't easy. I had a lot of false stops. "Tell you what," I say. "I'll buy you some Nicorette."

He bites his bottom lip, releases it. "And a pack to hold me over till the gum kicks in."

I squint at him, considering. "You got rid of everything else, like you said?"

"Yeah."

He doesn't flinch. My grandson's either an expert liar or he's telling the truth. I start to ask if that includes the stuff in his duffel lining, just to make sure, then push aside my doubts and choose to believe him. "Okay, it's a deal. But I'm only going to give you a couple from the pack and throw the rest out."

"Four." He raises his brows.

"Three." I tap my forefinger against my mouth. "And we eat healthy tonight."

Rolling his gaze to the roof of the car, he moans, "Do we have to?"

"You want a cigarette, or not?"

"Okay, whatever. If I have to eat tofu and bean sprouts, I will. But I don't have to like it."

We check into an old-fashioned, park-in-front-of-your-door motel on Route 66 then walk to a nearby diner so Nick can smoke and not stink up my car. The cigarette's gone before we reach the neon-lit restaurant.

Nick lucks out; not a single item on the menu is prepared with tofu or bean sprouts and the only salad listed is made with nutritionless iceberg lettuce. I use that as an excuse to cheat and eat high-fat for a change.

For the first time since we met, Nick and I are relaxed with one another. Over and over, we retell the pit-bull story. My version. His. We laugh that Tor's owner was more scary-looking than the pit bull. And we lose it all over again each time we reach the part where the woman called the dog a "son of a bitch."

On the walk back afterward, the desert air smells crisp and clean. I feel as if I've lost two hundred pounds off the top of my head, like I could float all the way back to the motel. Even Nick smoking the second cigarette doesn't drag down my spirits.

At the motel, I call Warren while Nick showers.

"You sound happy," he says.

"I am." I lie back against the pillows, close my eyes and twist my engagement ring round and round on my finger. "Tomorrow I might be right back to square one with him, but tonight was a gift. I'm going to enjoy it while I can."

Warren tells me he's glad, but apprehension still tinges his voice. I wish I could assure him that I'll be home soon and everything will be like it was between us. It frightens me that those words seem impossible for me to speak. I will go home soon. Things will be the same. Why is that so hard to say?

When Nick's out of the bathroom, I hang up and we watch a rerun of *The Matrix*. I fell asleep the first time I rented it. Too weird. Too much fantasy. Too many people performing impossible feats. But Nick's enthusiasm for the story is contagious and, from his perspective, I see it differently.

Nick falls asleep quickly after it ends, but my mind's too busy reliving the day to do the same. I dig my book light out of my suitcase, my reading glasses out of my purse, then choose one of Sarah's journals.

July 15, 1992

Dear Diary,

Why can't I stop thinking about the mystery mother? That's what I call her now in my mind. The woman who gave me life then gave me away. Growing up, I thought of her sometimes. On my birthdays, mostly. Or when I'd curse my red hair and this awful white skin that burns if I stand under a bright lightbulb. Or when I'd struggle with something like sewing, which I hate and Mom loves, and I'd look up and catch her watching me with sad eyes. Every time that happened, I'd think maybe I didn't turn out to be the sort of daughter she and Dad had hoped for.

Lately, the mystery mother creeps into my mind almost every day, though. Especially in the evenings when Nicholas and I do the bedtime routine. I wonder if she had more kids, or did she miss all this magic? The scent of soap on clean fingers and toes peeking out of soft pajamas. Giggles and complaints. Snuggling in to play little bunny foo-foo. Squeals... "Do it again, Mama! Again!" Yawns. Chubby fists rubbing droopy eyes. Toes sweet as cherry pie wiggling against my thigh, cozy and safe beneath the covers. Warm hugs and wet kisses. "A song, Mommy..." *Somewhere out there beneath the pale moonlight*...my heart spilling out with the melody.

I stand at the foot of Nick's bed, tired, content, watching him sleep, and I know that just this one simple moment makes everything worth it. The times, lots of them, when he isn't so sweet. When he throws temper tantrums or marks crayon on the walls or won't give me a second of peace. Postponing college. No money for anything extra. My crappy job and this shitty apartment. The lengthening stretch of time between phone calls from old friends. Only great books to keep me company in bed.

My son aggravates me one minute and amazes me the next. Makes me proud then makes me want to lock myself in the bathroom, turn on the shower full blast and stand under it for hours. He is everything wonderful and difficult in my life, who I am, the reason I'm on this earth.

What did she want that could've meant more? ~Sarah

I go to the bathroom to splash my face with water and pull myself together. Why did I read the journal tonight of all nights? My joy over this one good evening with Nick was so shiny and pure. Now guilty feelings tarnish that joy.

The cold water is harsh against my cheeks, but I don't warm it. I don't want to comfort myself; I want to sting, to force myself to face the hard questions. Questions like, would my daughter have been better off with me instead of the Pearsons? Did I opt for the easy way out? Convince myself I was making the right decision for my baby when really I was just afraid to raise her alone?

Anger at the Pearsons rages through me. I let my parents convince me that the agency would place my daughter with a couple capable of giving her so much more than I could, emotionally, as well as materially. Instead they made Sarah feel insecure. I tell myself that my anger is unreasonable. Despite any shortcomings they may have had as parents, the Pearsons still gave her more than I did.

As for Sarah, surely she struggled with the same concerns I did when she was pregnant with Nick. She made a different choice, and it came with heartaches just as my choice did. I've glimpsed a good soul beneath Nick's tough façade, but he has anger stored away inside of him that I suspect was there even before his mother died. I wish I knew why.

Turning off the water, I stare at myself in the mirror. Sarah found her identity through her son. *He is everything...who I am....* Is something vital missing at my core? Something that most mothers possess that, if I had it, too, would not have allowed me to walk away from my child?

I blink at my reflection. In the lines of my face, I see so much life. Falling in love for the first time, losing that love. Years of trying and failing and trying again. Dreams captured, dreams unfulfilled. Hopes for a lost lover, a lost child. Imagining, time after time, the sight of that lover's long hands cradling, so gently, the new life we made together. The three of us a family.

Startled by my thoughts, I step back, turn away from my gaze in the mirror. I know why I can't say the words Warren wants to hear, the words I so desperately want to speak. I'm still imagining that family. I never stopped. But that's crazy, isn't it? Insane. It isn't true. It's been too long. No one in their right mind clings to a teenage dream for thirty-six years.

I turn out the bathroom light then make my way to the foot of Nick's bed where, like Sarah used to do, I watch him sleep.

Our daughter is gone, Sonny's and mine. I missed my chance to answer her questions about me, about her father. To make her understand that I loved her, despite the choice I made. I missed my opportunity to know her, for her to know me, to know Sonny; I can't change that. The three of us will never be a family.

I walk to the head of Nick's bed, pull the sheet over his shoulder, making him stir.

Was Warren right? Am I using Nick as an excuse to see Sonny again? Clinging to an old dream, no matter how foolish it is?

Or, if that's not the case, if things work out and I do leave Nick with Sonny and go on with my life, is that really in his best interest, or just another easy out for me?

After all these years, the questions haven't changed. Only the child is different.

My grandson is alive. It's not too late for him.

CHAPTER 9

*W*e take our time the next day, and the next. Nick's attitude shift is as sweet, soothing and welcome as cool rain on a blistering summer day. With each passing mile, he talks more, telling me stories about his friends in Seattle, school, his hockey team. I'm not sure if the change in him is spurred by nervousness over the fact we're nearing our destination, by our recent carnival adventure, or both.

After days of indifference, now he wants to stop at every site along the way, small or large, interesting or ridiculous. We visit the Grand Canyon, Native American trading posts, a wigwam village, a rattlesnake farm. All fine with me. The truth is, I'm nervous, even if he isn't.

Now that we're finally starting to know each other, enjoy one another's company, I fear what adding Sonny to the equation might do to our newfound, fragile trust. Will Nick retreat again behind his anger? Pull the tough, impenetrable shell around himself?

Long after we cross the border into New Mexico, long past Albuquerque, the Beamer starts to stutter and stall. I pull over and stare out at the flat, desolate landscape. If this isn't the middle of nowhere, it should be.

Slapping the steering wheel, I reach for my cell phone, and sigh. "I'll call Triple A."

Nick opens his door. Warm, dry air sweeps into the car. "Let me take a look first."

Though I'm fairly sure we're wasting time, I join him under the hood where I stare into the mysterious maze of wires, pipes and tubes. "It's okay, Nick. They'll tow us to a garage in the little town up ahead. The last sign said we're about thirty miles out." I take off my sweatsuit jacket, tie the long sleeves around my waist.

Ignoring me, Nick walks to my door, reaches through the open window and pops the trunk. Then he goes back and takes out a tire tool. He returns to the maze under the hood and starts tapping the tool against something.

Parched wind whips hair into my eyes as I pace the ditch. Vehicles whiz past on the highway. After less than five minutes, Nick pokes his head around the hood and yells, "Try it now."

Back in the car, I turn the key in the ignition. The engine purrs to life.

Nick closes the hood, wipes his hands on his jeans then puts the tire tool back in the trunk. He comes around to the passenger door and climbs in, grinning. "Am I good, or what?"

"Where'd you learn to do that?"

"My grandpa. We'll still want to stop in the next town and have the fuel filter replaced."

Sadness sifts through me. It should've been Sonny teaching Nick to work on cars. Sonny was good with his hands, at building things, repairing them. He could have taught Nick so much. I think they would've loved each other. I hope it's possible they still might, that they'll connect at first sight without the awkwardness Nick and I suffered. If only Nick doesn't close himself off again.

Switching on the blinker, I pull back onto the highway. "So, you and your grandfather liked to tinker on cars together?"

"More like he tinkered and I got ordered around to hand him tools and stuff."

I laugh. "You were, what, twelve when he passed away?"

"Yeah."

"You must miss him."

The length of his pause implies a complicated relationship. I'm starting to believe no other kind exists.

"Yeah, I miss him. I mean, it's not like we were best friends or anything, but he was still my grandpa."

And, from what I've gathered, the only real male influence in Nick's life. "You two didn't get along?"

"Sometimes we did. He didn't talk much, but he could be cool. He came to my games and stuff. A lot of the time he just acted all irritated with me for no reason. I think it had something to do with my dad."

"Why would you think that?"

He shrugs. "I heard Mom yelling at him once for taking out his anger at my dad on me."

The picture of Paul Pearson forming in my mind is not the same jovial, softhearted man who, over the years, I'd envisioned raising my child. Last night's irritation toward him and his wife returns.

"Did you ever meet your dad?" I ask. I'm glad Nick brought up his father. I've wondered about the man Sarah talks about in her journals. Gary Bowers. He left her, like Sonny left me.

He shakes his head. "Mom didn't like to talk about him. All

123

my grandparents would say was that he was no good and I was better off without him. For a long time, I had this story all made up in my mind that he wanted to be with me, but Mom was hiding me from him." Nick blushes and sputters a self-depreciating laugh. "When I was twelve, right before my grandparents died, I got really mad at her one day when she wouldn't answer my questions. She finally told me she didn't know where he was, but that his parents still lived in Seattle."

"Did you see them?"

"Yeah. After Mom told me their name, I looked the address up in the phone book. I rode over on my bike. They only lived about two miles away." He stops, frowns. "All my life they'd been that close to me and I didn't even know it. When I told them who I was, they said if I was after money, they didn't have any. Then they told me they hadn't seen or heard from my dad in years. That was it. They didn't even invite me in." He turns to look out his window.

My chest aches with sorrow for him. "That must have been tough."

Nick's voice hardens. "I hated Gary Bowers after that. He abandoned me and Mom. He hurt her." He turns to the side window, his jaw set, the muscle there jumping. I begin to understand the source of all his pent-up anger. "Grandma kept telling me to pray about it and get my heart right."

"Did you?"

"Why would I pray to some god that doesn't exist?"

I relate to his disillusion with God, the universe, life. I know, firsthand, the kind of pain that births cynicism and doubt. "Are you sure about that, Nick?" I don't ask to shame him; I've struggled with the same question since the day I gave up Sarah. Maybe even before that. When Sonny disappeared from my life.

"If God does exist, I don't want anything to do with him. *He* abandoned us, too." Nick's eyes are as glassy as green marbles when our gazes meet, as hard as the first time I saw him. "He let Mom die."

Dean's Gas and Auto Repair looks like something straight out of Mayberry, only minus Gomer and Goob.

"I've got a couple of cars ahead of you," the mechanic says, twirling a toothpick between his lips with grease-stained fingers. "There's a coffee shop on the next block. You might want to grab a cup of joe and check back here in, say, an hour to an hour and a half."

Nick smacks his Nicorette and eyes the display of cigarettes behind the register with longing.

"Don't get any ideas." I nudge him with my elbow.

He makes a pitiful face. "This gum isn't cutting it."

"Give it some time." I nudge him again. "Come on. Let's go get something to eat. Maybe greasy food will take your mind off smoking."

Nick pulls some change from his pocket. "I want a candy bar for dessert. And I want to get my duffel from the car before we go."

Outside to coffee shop, a small mutt so skinny I can count every rib scavenges for crumbs in the gutter alongside a parked motorcycle. Nick slips his duffel bag off his shoulder and sets it on the sidewalk then squats a few feet from the dog. "Come here, boy."

Looking up, the mutt growls low in his throat.

"Watch it, Nick. Our luck with dogs this trip hasn't been the best."

"Animals love me. That pit bull was after you, not me." Nick tears the wrapper off the candy bar, breaks off a bite and holds it out. "He's wearing a collar. You think he's lost? He looks half-starved."

I step back. After Nick's comment about the pit bull's dislike of me, I'm as wary of this dog as he looks to be of us. "I don't think dogs are supposed to eat chocolate."

"There's no chocolate in this." He clicks his tongue. "Only peanuts and caramel."

The dog inches over, his head low. He sniffs the candy before snatching it from Nick's hand. No time wasted chewing for this guy; the bite goes down whole. Then the dog licks Nick's fingers.

Nick breaks off another chunk, offers it to him again.

Just as the dog takes it from his hand, the coffee-shop door opens. A stocky man steps out and starts for the cycle. He looks to be in his thirties, has a shaved head, and wears sunglasses and a leather jacket. Swearing, he stops alongside Nick and kicks the mutt. With a yelp, it darts away. "Stupid, worthless piece of shit."

Nick bristles. "Hey, I gave it to him."

"He don't need to get in the habit of eating other people's food."

"He's yours?"

The biker slips off his sunglasses. "Yeah, why?"

"Doesn't look like you want him getting used to eating, period. Look at him. He's starving."

The man's eyes narrow. "Mind your own business, asshole."

The back of my neck prickles. "Let's go, Nick."

126

Ignoring me, he juts his chin at the dog's owner. "You get some kind of thrill hurting defenseless things?"

Ten meaty fingers grab Nick's T-shirt collar.

The mutt growls; the hair along his rigid backbone stands on end.

I move a step closer. "Let him go."

Still holding Nick by the collar, the biker looks down at the snarling dog and kicks it again. "Can it, mutt." When he glances up, Nick slams him in the nose with a fist.

Chaos erupts. Nick and the man blur into a tangle of flailing arms and legs and curses. Sunglasses fly through the air. The dog barks. I run around in circles screaming, "Stop it! Stop!"

People emerge from the coffee shop and huddle around the doorway, some whispering, others yelling taunts.

When the two finally back apart for air, I wedge myself between them, my blood pumping and my skin tingling like I've been hit by a thousand needles. "That's enough."

Nick spits blood on the sidewalk.

The bald guy's face is crimson and his nose is starting to swell. "Move, bitch, or you're gonna get hit," he growls.

Reaching around me, Nick grabs at him. "Don't you—"

"Ow!" The man looks down. The growling dog nips at his ankles. He stoops, grabs a handful of fur, slings the whimpering animal toward the coffee shop.

My fingers clench; my nails dig into my palms. When he stands to full height again, I swing. The diamond in my engagement ring connects with his swelling nose.

Suddenly, I'm in the center of a tornado. Wrath and adrenaline surge through my veins, numbing me to any pain. I swing my arms, scratch and gouge. I'm not sure how long this goes on before the sound of a siren in the distance sends rationality screeching back into my brain.

Oh, God...the police...I could get arrested...go to jail....

And then a far worse possibility hits me. *The police...Nick's duffel bag.* It's on the sidewalk. A couple of feet away. Why did he take it from the car? Is his stash still inside?

According to Nancy Pacheco, Nick already has two strikes on his record. What happens at strike three? A juvenile detention center? It terrifies me to think what might become of him if that happened.

The siren's wail intensifies. Dodging a fist, I blink to clear my vision. I grasp Nick's arm and tug. "Let's get out of here." He keeps on swinging. "Nick! Let's go!"

My words finally register with him. Nick lunges for his trampled duffel bag, and we take off in the direction of Dean's Gas and Auto.

Glancing back, I see a squad car stop and two cops get out. One approaches the biker, the other starts after us. I grasp Nick's arm and stop. What's come over me? Driving across country knowing pot might very well be in my car. Getting into a fistfight. Running from the police. Warren will think I've lost my mind.

I think I've lost my mind.

A possession charge will be bad enough. All we need is another charge for evading arrest.

Turning, I face the cop.

Five minutes later, the biker, cursing about the condition of his nose, sits handcuffed in the front seat of the police car, while Nick and I lean against it and watch one of the officers dig through the duffel bag.

I look at my grandson and try to read his expression,

desperate to believe I wasn't wrong about him. He seems angry, but doesn't appear to share my terror. I hope that's not because this is familiar territory for him.

"Nothing here," the cop says to his partner, stuffing Nick's things back into the bag.

My relieved exhale brings Nick's head around, and we share a knowing glance. I see I-told-you-so in his eyes. Or maybe it's pride.

"Wouldn't hurt for all three of them to spend some time behind bars cooling off while we check for outstanding warrants," the other cop says. He guides Nick and me into the backseat then slides in beside us.

As the other officer drives us to the station, I lean back, close my eyes and sigh. Another first. I've lived fifty-two years, even survived the turbulent sixties and seventies, without doing jail time. But after only one week with Nick, I'm headed for the slammer.

The jail has only two cells. They're side by side, separated by a wall. The police officer locks the bald guy in the first one and puts us in the other. Ours is already occupied by a woman on a cot. Despite her coal-black hair, miniskirt and low-cut, threadbare blouse, she looks close to eighty.

The bars make a sickening clang as they close. "Better if you two share with Cookie." The cop nods in the direction of the biker's cell. "Those two have a history, and it isn't pretty."

The biker next door waits until the officer leaves and then yells obscenities at Nick and me.

"Hey, it's not so bad," the old woman says in a sandpaper

voice when she sees my face, which is probably tinged green, if it looks anything like I feel. "All the comforts of home." She sweeps an arm toward the cot, the toilet in the corner.

Nick sits at the opposite end of the cot from the woman while I start to lean against the wall then think better of it when I notice the vulgarities scribbled there. I stand in the middle of the cell, my arms crossed, eyeing my grandson and feeling like I might throw up. I suppose this is proof I was right, that I'm not fit to raise him. I should've stopped the fight, not joined in. For the first time since I moved out of my parents' house more than three decades ago, I feel completely powerless and out of control.

The woman pulls off a platform shoe, exposing her bare foot. The thick nails on her twisted toes are covered with chipped, sparkly blue polish. She rubs her sole and mutters, "Bunions...they're an occupational hazard, ya know?"

I glance up into her wrinkled, over-rouged face, hoping my disgust doesn't show. "What do you do?"

"Hook."

"Rugs?" I ask hopefully.

"No, hon." She winks. "Not rugs."

Nick turns and stares at her, his mouth open.

"Only one of my profession left in this town. Man wants a little pleasure around here, he pays me a visit."

"And brings two paper bags with him," the biker next door yells. "One to put over his head and one to barf in."

"That you, Crow?" Cookie calls back, her voice raspy.

"Yeah, it's me. How'd you know?"

"I smell ya."

"Hey, what're you in for this time?" he growls. "Some poor

sucker file a complaint against you for harassment? Cookie has to beg for business and still can't get no takers."

"Shove it, Crow."

"It's been a dry twenty years, ain't that right, Cookie? She gets herself thrown in here for the free meal."

The old streetwalker holds up her middle finger and jabs it toward the wall separating the cells. "If his prick was one tenth the size of his mouth he'd be steppin' on it." She raises her voice. "But, that's one problem you don't got to worry about, right, Crow? Not by a long-shot. I oughta know."

"In your dreams," he calls back.

She stands, walks to the wall and pounds on a brick until one end of it starts to shift. "You two mother and son?"

"I'm his grandmother," I say.

"I got me a grandson out in Vegas. Turned eighteen this year. Same birthday as me 'cept I turned sixty-seven." With the brick pried free, she pulls out a crumpled pack of cigarettes and a lighter. "His mama ain't let me around him since he was a baby. But I'm saving up to go out and pay him a visit now that he's growed up and can decide for hisself about me."

She lays the brick on the floor and returns to the cot.

"Mind if I bum one of those?" Nick asks, avoiding my eyes.

"Sure, hon."

They light up, filling the cell with the biting scent of menthol.

On legs that feel like two soggy sponges, I walk to the cot and face them. I reach for Nick's cigarette. He draws his hand away. "I'll give it back. I just want to see if it still calms my nerves like it used to." Right now, I'm desperate to relax.

His forehead lifts as he passes the cigarette to me. "You smoked weed *and* cigarettes?"

"I was young and stupid once, too." I take a drag and immediately choke on the smoke as it burns a pathway down to my lungs. I hand the cigarette back. "Well—" Waving the smoke away, I cough again. "I definitely made the right decision quitting. Someday, you'll be happy you did, too."

Cookie leans in, her droopy, painted face alert now. "You say you got weed?"

"No, we don't." Her animation fizzles as I shift back to Nick. "Speaking of which, I'm proud of you."

He reddens. "How'd you know it was in the duffel?"

"I checked your bags the other night."

"And you left it there?"

"You said you'd get rid of anything you had, and I said I trusted you to do it."

"But you weren't sure. I could tell you were freaking out when that cop was searching it."

"You've given me quite a few reasons to doubt you lately."

His brows lift. He looks away. "Yeah, I guess so."

"I don't doubt you anymore."

Blushing, he meets my gaze. He looks proud. And more than a little embarrassed about it. Another baby step. We're slowly bridging the gap.

Nick's face breaks into a grin. "Hey, you've got a mean right hook for a—" He pauses.

"For an old lady?" I ask, smiling back at him.

"For a grandmother."

He doesn't say *my* grandmother, but the acceptance is there, finally, between us. His acceptance. Mine. I thought having a grandchild would make me feel old, but Nick surprises me. Most of the time, he makes me feel young again. Or at least makes me remember how it was to be young.

When we hear the door at the end of the hall open, Nick follows Cookie's lead and stamps out his cigarette. She gathers the butts and quickly stuffs all the evidence into her hiding spot before replacing the brick.

Half a minute later, the officer appears, munching nuts from a bag. He sniffs the air. "Hand 'em over, Cookie."

She shoots him a grin that might look coy if not for her missing front teeth. "And what if I don't? You'll strip-search me?"

Swallowing, he makes a face, like he ate a rancid pecan. "No such luck, doll."

She cocks her head. "Either way, I ain't giving you nothing. You want 'em, you'll just have to find 'em."

The officer motions to Nick and me. "You two can go if you want to pay the fine."

I have just enough cash to cover the amount he quotes with twenty dollars left over. When he opens the cell door, Nick and I step out and he closes it again.

"Good luck, Cookie." I stick my remaining twenty through the bars. "For your Vegas fund."

She takes it. "Mighty nice of you."

"I hope you're reunited with your grandson soon." *It will change your life,* I want to say. I hope for the better.

Her blue-shadowed eyes mist over. "Me, too, hon. Me, too."

When we arrive at Dean's, the car is ready. We waste no time leaving. On our way out of town, we pass the coffee shop where the fight occurred. The mutt still sits on the sidewalk beside Crow's cycle. He lifts his head and looks at us.

Nick rolls down his window. "Stop."

"Nick—"

"Just for a second. *Please.*"

Ignoring my better judgement, I pull to the curb. Nick opens his door and whistles the dog over. He looks across at me. I shake my head. "We can't."

"Why not?"

"Because…we just can't."

Nick turns and slaps his leg anyway. The mutt jumps into the car at his feet then onto the seat between us.

Drumming my fingers against the steering wheel, I look from the dog to Nick. Then, throwing common sense out the window, I take off.

I cast nervous glances in the rearview mirror, my mind conjuring all sorts of outlandish scenarios. I imagine the police coming after us, sirens blaring, stopping us, then saying they made a mistake. They did find an outstanding warrant on Nick, and they're placing him under arrest. I imagine a furious Crow trying to run us off the road with his cycle to get his dog back.

Laughter bubbles out of me as the events of the past couple of hours hit home. It's been a long time since I've been as frustrated, taken as many risks, or had as much fun as I have on this trip.

Nick frowns at me. "What's so funny?"

"I was in a fistfight. I went to jail."

He grins.

I make a face at the dog. "Ugh. He stinks."

He strokes the animal's matted back. "At the next town we'll buy shampoo, and I'll give him a bath."

"Where?"

"We'll find a place. I'll borrow someone's water hose."

The dog gazes up at me and thumps his tail against the seat. I swear he's smiling. Warming to him, despite the putrid smell of his panting breath, I say, "Buy him a toothbrush, too." I pinch my nose. "Lord, that's enough to knock someone out. Or wake them up, I'm not sure which."

Nick reaches into his pocket and pulls out a plastic container of Listerine breath strips. "This should take care of that." He peels off a square, holds the dog's jaw and inserts the transparent square into his mouth. The tape sticks to the dog's tongue, and he licks the air and whines, trying to spit it out, bringing Nick and I to tears of laughter.

"What should we call him?" I ask.

"How about Sly? That was pretty sly of him, the way he won us over and escaped that asshole."

"Sly." I look at the dog, try the name on for size. "I like it. Would you put him in back for a while? He may be cute, but he could stand to wear a different cologne."

Nick lifts Sly over the front seat and into the back where he promptly curls up and goes to sleep.

"We need dog food, too," I remind Nick. "I hope the motel in Mesquite Bend allows pets. There's only one motel there, did I tell you that? We should make it in tonight. It'll be too late to see Sonny, but there's no sense staying somewhere else since we're this close."

Nick turns to the window, rubbing his palms up and down his thighs. "What was he like?"

"Who?"

"The redneck." He faces me again. Uneasiness tugs his brows together. "I know it's been a long time since you saw him, but how was he when you knew him?"

Nervous, too, I smile at him before returning my focus to the road ahead. "In some ways, Sonny was like you." I blow out a long breath. "He was so young the last time I saw him. Only eighteen. I was sixteen."

I let that sink in, the fact that I was his age when I conceived his mother. I hope he'll finally realize I wasn't that different than he is. That I can relate to and understand him. That I also made mistakes.

"Sonny loved animals, like you obviously do. And he was good with them, like you are, too." I tell Nick about my dad's cranky German shepherd and how Sonny charmed him. "He wanted a dog, but he couldn't have one because he lived in an apartment while he was working to save money to go to school."

I explain how Sonny was shaped by the times of his and my generation, by growing up during the politically charged sixties. I describe the way he dressed.

"So he was a hippie?" Nick asks.

"I suppose some people thought of us as hippies, but we weren't *true* hippies. Hard-core ones, I mean. We didn't go around barefoot all the time or live in a commune and spend our days smoking dope and growing our own food or anything like that." I laugh. "I guess we were on-the-fringe hippies, if that makes sense."

Nick listens as I try to explain how Sonny hated the war, but pulled for the soldiers fighting it. While I talk, I wonder if I'm irrational to expect he might understand my generation any more than I understood my parents'. The times I speak of are as foreign to him as Janis Joplin. And maybe that's the way it's meant to be.

"Most of all, Sonny was gentle and one of the friendliest

people I ever met before or since. He was so funny and spontaneous. He loved a good time."

Amusement flickers across his face when I tell him how we took off to Woodstock on the spur of the moment, how we didn't call my parents to tell them until we were far enough away that they wouldn't come after us. "Now that I'm older, I know it was a really irresponsible and insensitive thing to do." I wiggle my brows and laugh. "But it was a blast, too. It was crazy there. An experience I'll never forget. So many things…"

Remembering, I shake my head. "There was no place to bathe except a lake. Sonny didn't think twice about going in stark naked, surrounded by a bunch of other skinny-dippers." I don't mention that he wouldn't let me do the same. That he found a more secluded spot and shielded me with a blanket while I bathed and laughed at him.

"What happened to him?" Nick asks. "After you two split up?"

"I don't know. I haven't heard from him since."

I decide he doesn't need to hear about Sonny's quick exit from our relationship. I don't want him negatively judging the man he'll soon meet for something that occurred so long ago. I don't want to judge Sonny, either. I'm sure he had his reasons.

I want so much to believe that. But I've held on to my anger at him for so long, it's difficult letting go of it.

Nick clears his throat. "What if he doesn't want me?"

Though I'd never tell Nick, he voices my own fear. What would Sonny's rejection do to his psyche? The boy has already lost every important person in his world. But, somewhere along the road, I've also begun to worry about what will happen if Sonny *does* want Nick. Will he be any more suited to raise our grandson than I am?

I tell myself I should've thought all this through before we started on this trip. Taking off to see Sonny was a knee-jerk reaction to Nick's arrival in my life; I know that now. So many emotions wrapped up in that decision. Fear. Bitterness. The need for answers.

"It's what *you* want that matters most, Nick. If you decide you don't want to stay with Sonny, or he's not up for it, don't worry. We'll work something out."

"You keep saying that. We'll work something out. We'll go to plan B. What does that mean?"

No air seems to exist in the car at all; it's hard to breathe. "It means you can always stay with me. I thought you knew that."

Nick stares at me in a way that indicates he doesn't quite trust that I'm telling him the truth. But for the first time since he arrived at my house, I know it could work, us living together; I'd like it to work.

I'm still afraid. Terrified. But over the past few days, I've discovered a hidden side to my grandson. He's planted a seed in my heart and it's starting to bloom like the daisies on Sarah's journal. It feels like hope.

Or love.

CHAPTER 10

The Cozy Quilt, Mesquite Bend's one motel, has five rooms and no cars in the small parking lot. Since the town's population is two hundred seventy-seven and there's no major highway nearby, I'm surprised it stays open.

Nick sits in the car with Sly while I brave the blustering wind and blowing dust to go into the office and pay for a room.

According to Maureen Ingram, the Cozy Quilt proprietor, the only place to eat in town is the Cowgirl Café, which specializes in bacon-and-egg breakfasts in the mornings, burgers at lunch and Tex-Mex at night. The place is about to close, she says, though it's not yet eight o'clock. We'd better "get a move on" if we want to "grab a bite."

Maureen hands me the key to room three. "Not to be nosy, but what brings you through Mesquite Bend?"

"I'm here to visit an old friend."

"Oh, really?" She props her forearms on the counter and leans toward me. "Who might that be?"

I hesitate. The last thing I want is for word to get out to Sonny that I'm here before I have time to plan my speech to him. But I need directions to his place, so I take a chance. "His name's Sonny McGraw. You know him?"

"Honey, I know everybody around here. How do you know Sonny?"

"We were kids together. Out in California."

"That right?" She shakes her head and chuckles. "Well, ol' Sonny's still a kid at heart. He's a rascal, that one."

I give her a conspiratorial grin. "Will you do me a favor and keep my being here a secret? I want to surprise him tomorrow, and I'd hate for word to reach him before I do."

Maureen winks. "Nothing like a good secret."

"I'll need directions to his house."

She pencil-sketches a map on an envelope and hands it to me before I return to the car.

Nick and I settle into our room then hurry down the block to the café. Along the way, we pass a small grocery with *Mercantile* written on the sign, a boarded-up gas station, a vacant lot full of tumbleweeds. Not far in the distance, a white water tower stands guard over the town.

We arrive at the café five minutes before closing.

"No problem," the skinny, prune-faced man behind the counter tells us. "I don't mind firing up the grill again." He brings us two menus.

As I open mine and scan the selections, I breathe in the homey aromas of hot grease, warm bread and strong coffee.

"So, you're here to surprise Sonny McGraw, huh?"

I jerk my head up, my face flaming.

The man's wink mimics the woman's at the motel. "Don't worry. Your secret's safe with me and Maureen."

I'm sure. And the rest of the town, too.

My cell phone rings midway through dinner.

"Ally?"

It's Warren. "Hi, honey."

"You okay? I missed your call last night."

I wince. How could I have forgotten to call him? And Teena, too? "Oh—I'm sorry."

"I tried to call, but you didn't pick up."

It occurs to me that I haven't thought about my business at all today. That I haven't checked my phone for messages. A sliver of uneasiness slices through me. "We're here. In Mesquite Bend."

A long pause. I hear his breathing, then he asks, "Have you seen McGraw?"

"Not yet. We just pulled in and we're eating. We'll go out to his place in the morning."

The silence stretches into awkwardness before Warren says, "I hope it goes well and you can come home soon."

I nibble my lower lip, turn to the window, away from Nick's curious gaze. "How are things with you?"

"Okay. I miss you."

"I miss you, too." Outside, I see Sly stick his head and both paws out the car window. "Oh, Nick," I say. "I think Sly's about to get out. You'd better go raise the window some more."

"Sly?" Warren says.

"We've acquired a dog. It's a long story."

"I can't wait to hear it."

A note of jealousy rings in Warren's voice, as if he feels left out. My heart squeezes. "Soon, I promise."

As Nick leaves the table, Warren and I exchange goodbyes then hang up, and I'm even more conflicted than before. I sense more separating us than mere highway miles. It scares me to realize how little I've thought of him today. The last couple of days, in fact.

All while Nick and I are eating, I tell myself it's just the anticipation of facing my past again that has me so off center, distracted from the things most important in my life. All the things other than Nick, that is. Warren. The Slender Pea. My staff.

Later, back at the motel, I call Teena, then Nick and I watch television until almost midnight. But long after we turn it off, I still can't sleep. Questions I've avoided the entire trip refuse to be ignored any longer.

Sonny and I are three times older than the last time we saw each other. What will he think of me? The way I look now? The person I've become? What I've done with my life?

Why do I care so much?

I squeeze my eyes shut. Will he even remember me? I can't deny that it would crush me, humiliate me, infuriate me, even, to find out that, after all the years I've spent trying to make sense of what happened between us, he never gave me a second thought. That he put me out of his mind completely.

Rolling over, I hug the pillow. Does Sonny have a wife? Children? Grandchildren other than Nick?

I want to turn my face into the pillow, scream out my frustration with myself that any of this worries me.

But it does worry me. Like it or not.

I wish I'd asked Maureen about him, to prepare myself for what I'm walking into. It never occurred to me until now that Sonny might have a family, that the lives of other people besides him could be affected by Nick's and my arrival.

I toss onto my other side.

Sly whines in his sleep at the foot of Nick's bed.

Sensing movement in the room, I open my eyes and see the door open. My heart jumps, but when the moonlight sweeps in, I see Nick slip out into the night.

Pushing to my feet, I follow him.

He stands outside the door, leaning against the wooden railing that runs alongside the walkway. The wind has lost its bluster; the breeze breathes warmth against my skin. Still, I have goose bumps.

"Nick?" I touch his shoulder, but he doesn't turn. "You okay?" Moving up beside him, I try to see his face. "What's wrong?"

A sob slips out of him and grabs hold of my heart. "I don't want to be here, Ally."

Ally. It's the first time he's called me anything. I wondered if he ever would; I didn't know what to expect. Grandmother? Grandma? Those names belong to someone else in this life. "Ally" is fine. Perfect, in fact. It brings us another step closer. We're almost there.

"Nick." I turn him toward me, embrace him.

His arms stay firmly at his sides. "I want her back," he chokes out. "For things to be like they were. I'd be different. Better." He sobs again, his shoulders shaking. "Sometimes I hate myself."

"Don't." Tears seep from my eyes. I ache for him. For his loss. For mine. "Don't say that. It wasn't your fault."

"I don't want to be here. He wouldn't want me around. Why would he? Nobody does."

Nick's arms finally circle my waist. I feel his face in my hair. And I know we've finally found one another. I hold on tighter. I don't want to let him go. Not ever. How did I think I could? "I want you around, Nick. I want you with me so much. More than anything."

"You're just saying that." His fingers press into my back. "Why'd Mom have to die?"

I pull away, clutch his shoulders. "I've always wanted you. I was just a coward. I was afraid I couldn't do it right. That I couldn't give you what you need." *The same fears I had when Sarah was born.* "But none of that matters anymore. We'll figure it out together. Both of us."

He rubs his eyes with the palms of his hands, and I can see he's embarrassed by his tears. "So, I can live in Portland with you?"

I lick my salty lips, smile and nod at him. "We don't even have to see Sonny McGraw. In the morning, we'll turn around and go back. We'll make a point to stop at all the sights we missed on the way over. Hopefully, not all the jail cells between here and home, though." I laugh.

He smiles a little, sniffs and shrugs. "We've come this far. I guess I should at least meet him."

Something flutters inside my chest. Anxiety. Relief. "If that's what you want."

My conflicting feelings butt heads again. Nerves insist I should leave the past alone. Curiosity demands answers to so many old questions.

"We'll drive out there in the morning. Then we'll go home."

It must've been at least three o'clock Monday morning when I sat next to Sonny on the ground listening to Crosby, Stills and Nash sing "Find the Cost of Freedom." I was more tired than I'd ever been. Tired, hungry and dirty.

And happy. So happy.

I laid my head on his shoulder and tugged our shared blanket around us. "Hold on to me, Sonny." Yawning, I closed my eyes.

His embrace tightened. His whisper tickled my ear. "I'll always hold on to you, Al. Always. No matter where I am."

If his voice sounded strange, I didn't notice. If his statement held deeper meaning, it didn't register. I never thought to analyze his words or question him. That would come soon enough.

Too soon.

I don't think we spoke on the way back to the tent. I barely remember that walk at all, only the warmth of the sleeping bag that had finally dried out, his arms safely around me, darkness and sleep.

The next morning, I awoke to Jimi Hendrix and an empty tent. Stretching and yawning, I slipped into my last clean T-shirt, then crawled out to find Karla, Chuck and Dale poking through a pile of blankets and trash. "Where's Sonny?"

They glanced at each other, avoiding my eyes.

"He took off." Dale held up a shoe then tossed it aside.

"Where to?" I touched Dale's arm. "Did he go get something to eat?"

Dale slid me a quick look. "I don't know. He talked to Chuck."

"He didn't tell me anything." Chuck cleared his throat. "Just that he had to split and I should make sure you get home. He made me promise to watch out for you."

Karla took my hand, but I jerked it back, as if her fingers burned as hot as my cheeks. "Why didn't you tell me, Karla? Why didn't you wake me up so I could stop him?"

"I wasn't here." She reached for me again, drew me to her, pity in her eyes. "Dale and I went to the lake to bathe."

"I don't understand." Shaking my head, I stepped back, scanned the people all around us, dread filling my chest, embarrassment. "How long?"

"About an hour ago," Chuck answered, without making eye contact.

"I don't understand," I whispered again.

I couldn't put only one name to what I felt. Panic. Confusion. Humiliation. I lunged at Chuck, shoving him backward. He'd betrayed me almost as much as Sonny. "You should've woke me up," I screamed at him. "Why didn't you?" I lifted my hand to strike him.

He caught my wrist before I hit his chest. Then he wrapped me in his arms, let me cry against him. "He asked me not to, Ally. I'm sorry."

Sorry. Not as sorry as me.

I wept hot tears onto his grainy shirt. So stupid. How could I have misjudged Sonny? He was everything...everything.

Despite the urgings of my friends, I refused to leave that day. And, though the concert was long over, I insisted we stay another night in the tent.

On Tuesday, beneath a gloomy, gray sky, I roamed the bedraggled, trash-strewn field like a number of other stragglers with no place to go, bewildered and dull-eyed, like shell-shocked survivors of an unnatural disaster, searching in the shadows surrounding the skeletal remains of speaker scaffolds and stages, beneath soggy piles of blankets and sleeping bags, around ghostly smoking fires of burning trash, looking for lost shoes, lost car keys, lost lovers. Remnants of reality in a suddenly surreal world.

"He's not here," Karla said for the hundredth time. "Sonny's gone. He's not coming back."

And she was right. Sonny never came back. Not to Yasgur's field that day. Not to his apartment in California later. Not to me.

Not ever.

Nick and I follow Maureen's pencil-sketch map past mesquite-dotted prairies, past dried-up creek beds, past grazing cattle and spinning windmills.

Barbed-wire fence and telephone poles line both sides of the two-lane highway. We don't talk; even Sly stays quiet. He sits between us, his nose lifted, as if he smells tension and anticipation hanging thick in the air.

At 10:00 a.m. a yellow sun beams bright above wispy white clouds in a sky so crystal-blue it seems unreal. Fitting, I think. This day seems unreal. In my rearview mirror, the miles unravel behind me, my last sight of reality. Out my front window, the blacktop road unfurls, a pathway into a dream. Just another imagined scenario. I've had hundreds before. Yet this one is different, somehow. In this dream, cool morning air rushes in through the open window, carrying us forward. *No going back,* it whispers. *This is it, this is real. Finally. Finally.*

All the years since that last day at Woodstock, everything that's happened since I heard his last words...*I'll always hold on to you, Al...no matter where I am...,* all the tears and the searching, the wondering and the anger, they all led me here. To this lonely turnoff onto a dusty, rock road. To a familiar scene I once described to Sonny while we held one another in a dark tent, in a life now so removed from mine I can almost believe it belonged to someone else.

There's a pasture with at least two grazing horses and another with more cows than I can count. A modern-looking, curved-top metal barn in the distance. A little white farmhouse with another barn, a big, old-fashioned red one, behind it. Chickens peck in a huge wire pen in the side yard.

I stop in the gravel drive alongside the house, behind a mud-splattered black truck. My heart pounds, my head feels dizzy, my knees are unsteady when I step from the car.

"Wait here." I lean down to look in at Nick. "I'll try not to take too long."

His pale face tells me he's nervous, too. "Don't hurry."

I climb the steps onto a porch with a bench swing at one end of it, a pot of droopy geraniums beneath a window, a welcome mat in front of the door. I knock, wait a minute, then ring the bell and wait some more.

Maybe he's not here, I think. Maybe I drove all this way, waited all this time and he's gone. On a vacation with the wife and kids. Or maybe he was tipped off about me coming by Maureen and the guy at the café and he packed up and moved in the middle of the night.

A sound rings out from behind the house, a sharp, clear *ping ping ping.* I take the steps down again, walk through the spring grass to the back of the house then across a stretch of less-green grass that leads to the barn.

Inside the open doors, a man works on something I can't make out, his back to me. As I near, I see he's barbed-wire thin and wearing a straw cowboy hat, jeans and boots. His sleeves are rolled up and he's swinging a hammer.

I step into the barn behind him. "Excuse me."

He lowers the hammer. Turning, he lays it down then removes his hat, revealing silver-gray hair cut close to his head. Hair that matches his handlebar mustache. His face is weather-worn and ruddy, the hands holding the hat, calloused, work-roughened and dry.

"I was wondering..." I clear my throat, try again. "I'm looking for Sonny McGraw?"

Deep lines etch pale fans into sunbaked skin beside the eyes staring back at me. *Squinting green eyes.* I look into them...and all the breath rushes out of my body, every muscle goes limp.

"Sonny," I whisper.

The mustache twitches. He blinks. His brows draw together. The hat slips from his fingers and falls to the floor at his feet.

"Al?" He steps closer, blurts an uncertain laugh. "Al, is that you?"

He takes my hands in his rough ones, both of them, turns and walks backward, drawing me out of the barn and into the light. For seconds, we stand like that, with our hands linked and our gazes caught.

"I don't believe it," he says at last. With a whoop of what sounds like joyful disbelief, he grabs me, lifts my feet from the ground and twirls me around. And all at once, we're both laughing. Laughing and hugging and twirling.

When we stop and step away from one another, awkwardness settles in and, like me, he appears to be at a loss for words. Still we can't stop staring at each other.

Chickens squawk, pulling my attention to the side yard where they peck, and then on to the pasture beyond. "All that's missing is the big, horny rooster," I whisper, my eyes filling. I turn to Sonny and see that his smiling eyes are also glossy with unshed tears.

"He's here somewhere," he assures me. "It wouldn't have been right without a rooster." He shakes his head. "How did you find me? Why are you here?" When I look away, he reaches for my hand again. "It doesn't matter. You're here." He nods toward the house. "Let's go inside. Get you something to drink. Did you fly into Amarillo or drive? Nothing's close to Mesquite Bend. You must be whipped." The words tumble out of him.

When he starts for the house, I pull back, my heart knocking unsteadily. "Wait. I brought someone. Someone I want you to meet. He's in the car."

Sonny's thumb snags the diamond on my finger. He looks down. "Husband?"

I shake my head. "I'm not married."

"Me, either." Lifting my hand, he takes a look. "Ah. That's some rock, Al." Again, he meets my gaze. "A fiancé, then."

"Let me run to tell Nick to give us a minute. There's something I'd like to talk to you about before you meet him. He can take the dog for a walk or something."

Curiosity narrows his eyes even more. "Sure."

I let go of his hand. "I'll be right back."

When Nick sees me, he and Sly get out of the car. Sly prances around, jumping up on Nick and yapping at the chickens. Before I reach them, I see Nick's attention focus on something behind me. When I look back, Sonny stands at the side of the house, watching us, wearing his hat again.

"Is that him?" Nick whispers.

"Yes."

"I told you he'd be a redneck." No resentment darkens his expression, only wariness.

"Take Sly for a walk while I talk to him," I say quietly. "Don't go too far, though. I'll be back out for you."

I meet Sonny on the porch, and he leads me to the door. He has a pronounced limp, I notice. One leg that's a bit stiff, as if the knee doesn't bend like it should. I wonder about it as we go inside.

The house is simple and plain, but clean and neat enough, especially for a bachelor. To the left of the entry, in the living room, there's a small television and a stereo, both set into a bookcase that fills one wall. The shelves of the case are stacked with CDs and an assortment of books—thick hardcovers and creased, worn paperbacks. On the opposite wall sits a brown sofa, the leather buffed smooth in spots from years of use, reminding me of an old saddle. There's a recliner covered in nubby green fabric, a knitted beige throw tossed over the back of it, a wicker rocking chair. TV trays sit beside each piece of furniture, serving as side tables.

Sonny takes a right into the kitchen and removes his hat to a peg on the wall. He sits me at a scarred oak table, then pours two cups of coffee from a pot on the stove.

"It's still warm," he says when he gives me mine. "I leave the burner on low. Bad habit of mine." Sitting across from me, he laughs and shakes his head. "I can't believe I'm looking at you. After all these years. I just can't believe it. My Al."

A fresh wave of emotion rises in me as I smile and stare back at him. The expression in his eyes is far warmer than the coffee. It answers many of the questions that tormented me last night. He gave me more than a second thought over the years. He didn't forget.

"I can't believe it, either," I tell him. And I can't get over how much he's changed. "You're a cowboy." I laugh. *My long-haired hippie lover.* "When I thought of you, I never imagined that."

Our eyes lock. *Yes, I thought of you, too. A million times. A trillion. Too many to count.*

Would I have recognized him if I passed him on the street, I wonder? Only if I had looked in his eyes. The old familiar spark's still there. Everything else has changed. Even his laughter and voice are different. Richer, deeper.

Turning, he glances out the kitchen window that looks over the driveway and front yard, where Nick chases Sly back and forth.

"Nice car," Sonny says. "A few steps up from the old Ford Tempo."

"I lost the Tempo."

He looks back at me. "Lost it?"

"At Woodstock." *Like I lost you. And a part of myself.* Heat flushes my face. Why did I bring that up? "Only for a while. We couldn't remember where we'd parked it. Chuck finally found it, though."

"Chuck." His laugh is short. "Wonder what happened to him? And the others." He seems to struggle to come up with their names.

"Karla and Dale."

"That's right." Now his face reddens, too. Maybe he reads my thoughts. *What else has he forgotten about that weekend?* Or maybe he remembers all of it and wishes he didn't.

Returning his attention to Nick and Sly in the yard, he grins and says, "No offense, Al, but don't you think the kid's a little young for you?"

I tilt my head. "I didn't say it was my fiancé waiting in the car. You just assumed."

"Who is he? Your son?"

"No, my grandson." When he turns to me, I take a deep breath. Then another. I hold his gaze. "He's our grandchild, Sonny. Yours and mine."

CHAPTER 11

Stunned. The word doesn't adequately describe Sonny's expression. It's as if he melts into the chair, diminishes, ages even more before my eyes. Emotions, raw and vulnerable, play across his face.

"Our – ?" He shifts to look out at Nick in the yard then back at me again, his head shaking slowly. He draws a breath so loud and shaky, I hear it. "What are you saying?"

"We had a baby." My voice quivers.

Sonny closes his eyes. He scrapes his fingers across his scalp, forehead to crown.

"A little girl."

"God, Al. Oh, Jesus."

"With red hair like yours. She was beautiful, Sonny. Perfect."

He opens his eyes and looks at me. "Where is she?"

"I was so young and scared. I didn't know if I could do it alone. My parents…they wanted me to place her for adoption. I didn't know what to do." I look down at my lap. "I gave her away," I whisper.

His chair legs scrape across the floor. Then he's sitting beside me, lifting my chin. There's no judgement in his eyes, only regret. "But she must've found you."

"No, Nick did. Less than two weeks ago. I didn't even know he existed until then. He said his mother—" A sob shudders out of me. "She died a month ago from breast cancer. He doesn't have anyone left. No family, except us. A friend has custody, but she and her husband don't want Nick. Not really. I met them. It's not a good place for him."

His face pales, and I regret that I told him everything so quickly. I can see it's almost too much for him to take in. Too cruel. Discovering you have a child one minute then losing her the next. I don't have to ask what he's feeling when he props his elbows on the table and cradles his face in his hands. I wait while he catches his breath and, when he lowers his hands again, I take the envelope of photographs from my jacket pocket and hand them to him, promising myself I'll be strong for his sake.

"Her name was Sarah," I say quietly as he spreads the pictures on the table in front of him. "Sarah Pearson."

It's no use. I cry along with him as he looks at each one. For our lost love, the daughter we missed knowing, the life we might've lived together.

"Nick gave me her journals, and I'm leaning a lot about her." He lingers over each picture a second time. A Third. "Daisies were her favorite flower."

He looks up. "You liked daisies."

"I still do." We smile at each other. "She loved movies, too. And all kinds of music. Rock, country—"

"Like me."

"And she enjoyed books."

He returns his attention to the photographs. Sarah at nine or ten years of age dressed as a pickle for Halloween makes us laugh through our tears. And, when Sonny studies her in prom dress and heels, grinning at the camera, he says, "What a knockout. I see you in her."

"I see you."

"But you have that same expression...and around her mouth..."

"She has your hair, though. Your coloring." I point at her image. "And your nose."

He looks closer. "She makes this nose look good."

Laughing, I squeeze Sonny's arm and wonder if this is how we would've been together at her birth. Proud parents. Amazed by our child. Searching for signs of ourselves and each other in her features, every smile, each expression.

"She found me through the adoption agency, but never contacted me," I tell him.

The kitchen window is open. A puff of breeze blows in through the screen. I hear Nick's whistle, Sly's answering bark.

After a while, Sonny restacks the photos and meets my eyes. In his, I see sorrow as weathered as his face. Not fresh, not born today from the news I brought. Sorrow that's as much a part of him as his crooked smile or his limp.

"What happened to Nick's father?"

"He left when he found out Sarah was pregnant."

Sonny blinks at me but doesn't avoid my gaze. "I was stupid, Al. A confused kid. But, I promise you, if I'd known about our baby—"

I stop his words with an upheld hand. "Please, don't. Not yet.

I can't talk about it." My throat feels too tight to swallow as I turn to the window. Arms crossed, Nick squints at the house while Sly darts around him, begging attention. "Nick hasn't had it easy. He's troubled in some ways after all he's been through. Who wouldn't be? But he's a good kid. He wants to meet you."

"I want to meet him." With a sniff and a smile, Sonny pushes back his chair and goes to the counter for a box of tissues. He offers them to me while wiping his face on his sleeve. "Ready when you are."

Seconds later, we take the porch steps down into the yard, side by side, then start for the graveled driveway where Nick tosses a stick for Sly. The dog takes off.

I make introductions.

Nick dusts his palms on his jeans, lifts a hand toward Sonny and says, "Hello, Mr. McGraw." They shake.

I'm suddenly so proud of him. He's come so far. Nick acts uncomfortable and wary, but the cocky coldness has vanished, taking the angry, resentful edge along with it. I'm glad he's making an effort not to cast blame, to put that all behind him.

"Glad to meet you, Nick. Call me Sonny." When the dog rushes up to them, he reaches down to pet him. "And who's this?"

"Sly," Nick says to him. "Me and Ally stole him from a biker."

Sonny looks back at me with a bemused expression. "I'll want to hear all about that."

He returns his attention to Nick, and I stand back and watch them, mesmerized.

"It's lucky y'all caught me at the house. I just came in from the pasture to pick up some tools and got sidetracked by a little job I've got goin' on." Sonny's body is as hard as the gravel beneath his boots. But the look in his eyes is as soft as the fluffy clouds overhead. All traces of tears are gone. He's animated now, and talking nonstop. His Texas accent amuses and fascinates me.

"When Al walked into the barn, I thought nothing could shock me more. Then she told me about you, and, well, let's just say, I was wrong. Two whoppers in one day. Two great surprises."

Nick doesn't seem to know how to respond to his new grandfather's open-armed welcome. It's strange to say, considering Sonny's abrupt, unforewarned exit from my life, but he was never one to sugarcoat a situation, to pretend, and he doesn't now.

"Other than your mom, I never had any kids. I sure wish I could've known her. Right now, I just feel damn lucky Al brought you so *we* can get to know each other." He looks at me. The crack in his voice is subtle; I doubt Nick hears it, but I do.

"Where do you live, Nick? Al and I didn't get around to that."

"I come from Seattle."

Sonny nods at me. "You, too?"

"I live in Portland. I own a café there."

"Don't happen to serve kumquats, do you?"

My heart dips. He does remember. Everything. Warmth spreads through me, inside and out.

"She probably does," Nick says, saving me from having to find my voice and speak up. "She doesn't serve much normal stuff, that's for sure."

"Let's head out back," Sonny says with a laugh, leading the way. "I'll show you around the place."

I lag a couple of steps behind, watching them together.

Listening. Sonny's limp is more pronounced than before. It saddens me to imagine the type of injury he must have endured to produce such a noticeable handicap.

"You ever been to Texas before, Nick?" he asks.

"Nope."

"So what do you think of it so far?"

"Not much."

Nick's open-mouthed stare tells me he's startled by Sonny's loud, heartfelt laugh. "I like your honesty," Sonny declares. "Sometimes newcomers can't see the Panhandle's beauty. But I'll make you a bet. Stick around here with me long enough and you'll grow to appreciate it. I did, anyhow. Prettiest sunsets and sunrises anywhere. Nothing to block the view. Sky as far as a man can see."

Midway to the barn, he slows to point out the pasture and tell us about the herd of four-hundred cattle he raises.

"Maybe you can convince Ally it wouldn't kill anybody if she sold hamburgers," Nick says with a hint of teasing in his tone. "Then you could sell her some beef for the Slender Pea."

"The what?" I hear the scowl in Sonny's voice.

"That's the name of her restaurant. The Slender Pea." They both laugh, like they're sharing a joke I don't get, and Nick adds, "I know. Pretty weird, huh?"

I'm enjoying their conversation. Even their teasing. Sonny handles Nick's arrival in his life so much better than I did. He's instantly accepted that he's a grandparent, taken the surprise in stride, even derives pleasure from it. The happiness I hear in his tone is too pure and natural to fake.

Sonny explains that, besides the cattle, he also farms. "Wish I could say I owned this land, but I only lease it. The owner gets a percentage of my profit. It's worked out for us both over the years. I'm not out to get rich, just do what I like doin'."

They reach the barn ahead of me. "Ever ride a horse?" Sonny asks Nick.

"Nope, but I'd like to."

"Well, what are we waiting for?"

"Really?" Nick perks up. "You mean I can ride today?"

"Don't know why not. How about you, Al? You want to? We could all three go."

"I've never ridden a horse, either, unless you count those ponies that walk in circles at carnivals. I doubt I could even climb on."

"I'll help you. I won't let you fall."

The same happiness I hear in Sonny's voice swells in me, unexpected. Something I can't explain. What a fool I must be to trust him completely, like I always did. He's given me every reason not to, and still I wouldn't hesitate to put my safety, even my life, in his hands.

"Sure," I answer. "Why not?" After running down an eighteen-wheeler, being chased by a pit bull and trading punches with a biker, riding a horse should be as easy as boiling water.

Sonny returns to the pasture to let his hired hands know he'll be "out of pocket," then we spend the entire day together. He gives Nick and me a two-hour riding lesson during which we see a small part of the fourteen sections of land he leases. Afterward, he makes ham sandwiches for himself and Nick, and peanut butter for me. We eat the sandwiches and drink lemonade at the picnic table beside the house. Then we walk to a small horse arena where he shows us how to throw a rope.

Throughout it all, Sonny talks, and I discover that the man has more tales of adventure than a public library.

"Once I met this kid when we were both hitchin' across Illinois," Sonny says, while Nick plays with the lasso and I sit nearby on the fence, watching.

Clearing my throat, I catch his eye and he adds, "Which was really stupid on my part, so don't get any ideas."

I smile at him, and he shifts back to Nick.

"Anyway, we ended up in this little town that had a water tower shaped like a catsup bottle. Painted like one, too. Biggest damn bottle of catsup you've ever seen. Must've been a hundred and fifty feet high or more. Well, we didn't have any money for a place to sleep that night, so we decided we'd climb up that tower and sleep on the deck, which is just what we did." He chuckles. "Another stupid idea. Middle of the night, here comes a thunderstorm. Big bolt of lightning strikes the tower and sparks go flying. Scares the you-know-what out of me, and I stumble backward over the railing."

Nick's eyes widen. "*Shit.*"

"That's what I said just before I caught hold of the railing with one hand, and this kid I'm with leans down and grabs my collar. But the rain's made the railing slippery, and I start to lose my grip."

I gasp. "Don't tell me you fell?"

"Is that how you hurt your leg?" Nick asks.

"No, but it almost ended up worse. My shirt ripped, and I was screaming and kicking and cussing up a storm, but just when my fingers slip completely, the guy grabs my other hand and, somehow or another, he has the strength to haul me up."

Sonny blows out a breath of relief and scratches his head. "Wish I could remember that kid's name. I still owe him a steak dinner."

"Man, you were lucky." Nick laughs, then asks, "How *did* you hurt your leg?"

Sonny cuts a glance to where I sit on the arena fence. "In the war."

My stomach drops. All the breath rushes out of me. Sonny fought in the war? Impossible.

"Vietnam?" Nick stops twirling the rope. "Ally told me you were against it."

"I was. But Uncle Sam didn't care about that. I got drafted, anyway. Didn't want to go, but what could I do? I had friends over there." He nods at the metal dummy practice steer sitting in the arena's center. "Give it another shot, kid."

My heart beats too fast as the puzzle starts fitting together, creating an image I never imagined. Vietnam. Is that why he left me? It still doesn't explain the way he disappeared without a word.

Adjusting his stance, Nick asks, "So what happened? You step on a land mine or something?"

"A mortar exploded. I got hit by shrapnel."

"Man." Nick shakes his head. "So'd you come home after that?"

"Yeah."

"Why doesn't your leg bend right? They couldn't fix it?"

Sonny doesn't look at me as he reaches down and knocks a fist against his knee. "It isn't real. I lost my leg," he says, matter-of-factly. "Here." Ignoring Nick's slack-jawed stare, he adjusts the boy's fingers on the rope. "Now, try it."

I feel like I've been kicked in the chest by one of Sonny's

horses. When Nick swings and throws, I see it all in a blur. He rings the metal steer's neck, but I'm the one choking, unable to breathe. I'm sick for Sonny, guilt-ridden about the scenarios I imagined as a young mother grieving the loss of our child. Him living a wild, carefree life without me. No worries, no responsibilities, when, really, he was off fighting a war. Lying in a hospital bed wounded and alone. Broken.

Whooping, Sonny slaps Nick on the back. "Nice one, kid. You're a natural. We'll have you on the rodeo circuit in no time."

"Excuse me." I jump from the fence and walk quickly across the arena, pressure building inside my chest. When I'm on the other side, I start running toward the house and don't stop until I reach the porch. I sit on the top step, lean forward, my arms crossed on my knees, my face pressed against them. *He went to Vietnam. He lost his leg. Oh, God. Oh, God.*

It's too much. All those years ago, while I was loving and missing him, hating and blaming him. Why didn't he tell me. Why?

Minutes pass before someone sits beside me and touches my hair.

"It's okay," Sonny says.

"It's not okay." I look up at him, my face wet with tears, my voice choked. "It isn't fair. It shouldn't have happened. Not to anybody. But especially not you." A sob seizes me. "Not you."

He wraps his arms around me. We rock back and forth. "It was a long time ago. I survived. I'm fine now, Al. I do okay."

"You knew, didn't you? You knew you were going to Vietnam when we were at Woodstock."

He doesn't say anything.

"I should've been there for you. I would have." I pull back, look into his eyes and whisper, "Why didn't you tell me?"

Before he can answer, I see Nick approach. He hangs back when he spots the two of us. I ease from Sonny's arms, wipe my eyes, stand. "It's been a long day. We should go back to the motel."

Sonny stands, too. Jams his hands in his pockets. "Don't leave until we've had dinner. Hell, get your things from the motel and stay here. I have an extra bedroom and the couch in the living room makes out."

"Thanks, but I don't think so." I need time away from him. Distance. To think about today, all that's happened, everything I've learned.

The space between his brows puckers. He looks past me. "Nick?"

Nick makes his way toward us, shifting his attention from Sonny to me. "If I go to the motel with you," he asks me, "can we come back here tomorrow?"

"Of course you'll come back," Sonny says.

I look at them both. Their expressions are identical, their green eyes brimming with hope and concern.

So much can change in just a few hours. Only last night, Nick couldn't wait to go back to Portland. Now he doesn't want to leave. Why does that surprise me? This isn't the first time my life's turned upside down in a blink.

"Yes." I lock gazes with Sonny. "We'll come back."

While Nick flips through a Rolling Stone magazine he bought on the road, I report in with Bev then call Teena.

"Allyson, finally. I tried to reach you all day but I couldn't get through."

"I was out in the country at Sonny's place. The reception must be bad. Bev said she had trouble, too. Is something wrong?"

"Only everything. Guy and Joleen called in with the flu. I couldn't get a hold of Vicky or Marie to fill in. You need to hire more people, Ally, I'm serious. When are you coming home?"

"Slow down. So what did you do?"

"Well, he told me not to tell you, but I'm going to. I called Warren."

"Warren? Why?"

"I didn't know what else to do. He came in, Ally. You should've seen him. That man took care of everything. He helped me cook, he worked the buffet line, he checked on tables, cleared the dishes. Everything."

I close my eyes and think of Warren. Then I think of Sonny and everything between us that's still unfinished. "I'll leave tomorrow."

"You'd better. Warren is a great guy. The best."

"Don't you think I know that?"

"They why are you out there chasing after some cowboy?"

"Is that what you think?"

"Well, it's Texas, isn't it? And you said the guy lives in the country."

"Just a minute." I hold my hand over the phone and look at Nick. "I'm going outside for some air," I tell him. He glances away from the magazine, nods, then returns his attention to the page.

Once outside, I lean against the railing. The air smells dusty. Crickets chirp. I wave away a fly. "I'm not here for me, Teena. I'm here for Nick."

"I hope you're sure about that, because I'd hate for you to make a big fat mistake. I'm worried about you."

"Well, don't be. Could we please get back to the café?"

"I wish you would."

Frustrated, I look up at the star-dotted sky. How can I leave so soon after what I found out today about Sonny? But how can I leave my business problems on Warren's shoulders, either? "So, let's figure out what you're going to do until I get there. Did you ever find Vicky or Marie? Can they fill in tomorrow and the next day?"

"Yeah, and I think Guy's feeling a lot better tonight, so maybe he'll be able to come in, too."

"Hey, I just noticed something. What happened to your lisp?"

"I took the stud out of my tongue."

"You did? Why?"

"I met someone today. He came in to the Pea and we went out for coffee this evening. He didn't like the way it felt when we kissed."

I smile. Teena's not one to waste time. "You've only known the guy one day and you removed the stud for him? He must be something."

"He is. I really like him. You'll never guess who it is." She pauses, then before I can respond, says, "Warren's son."

"Reid?"

"Yeah." Her voice sounds dreamy. "He's in med school in Seattle, you know? He did some time off and came by the café looking for his dad."

I hope she doesn't hear me snicker. I think of Teena's spiked hair, which is usually pink one week, blue or purple or green the next. I think of the tongue stud. The butterfly tattoo on her hip bone. The rose she probably has by now on her boob.

Marjorie, Warren's ex and Reid's mother, will pop a vein when she meets Teena.

After we say goodbye, I call Warren. "Why are you so good to me?" I ask, the second he picks up.

"Ally? What are you talking about?"

I stare down the road, past the Cowgirl Café's lit sign. Not a single vehicle out tonight. The silence is eerie. Surreal and bone-deep lonely. "I can't believe what you did today."

"Have you been talking to Teena? I told her not to say anything."

"Why wouldn't you want me to know?"

"Because you have enough on your mind."

"Warren..." I hurt to hold him. "I love you so much."

"I hope so."

"What do you mean, you hope so? You know I do."

For a minute he doesn't say anything, then he adds, "You need to call Bev. She said she hasn't heard from you in a couple of days, and she couldn't get through on your phone today."

"I talked to her a second ago."

"Good."

A door hinge squeaks. Down the way, Maureen, the motel proprietor, steps out of the office holding a broom. The porch light illuminates her as she sweeps dirt and leaves from the welcome mat.

"Tell me about your day," Warren says.

"I rode a horse, had a roping lesson, and was terrible at both."

Warren chuckles. "What about Nick?"

"He did better. A lot better."

"I guess McGraw was shocked to see you?"

"Yes. Of course, he would be. It's been a long time. He took the news about Sarah hard, but he handled finding out about Nick a lot better than I did. He's good with him. They get along well together. Nick's intrigued, I can tell." Why wouldn't he be? The truth is, I am, too. "You should see Sonny, Warren. He's a cowboy now. Not only does he farm and ranch, he ropes, rides a horse and wears boots and a great big hat."

"White or black?"

"What?" When his implication strikes me, I smirk. "Neither. It's straw."

"So, he's one of the good guys, but not *too* good."

"He's so different than he used to be," I say, ignoring Warren's sarcasm. "At least on the surface."

"Considering how much you used to love the guy, I can't say that I'm sorry to hear that. Does he have a family?"

"No. No wife or kids."

"I *am* sorry to hear *that*."

"Stop it, Warren." I take a deep breath, my emotions still so full they could easily spill over. "He served in Vietnam," I say quietly. "He lost a leg over there."

"Damn." Warren's voice holds compassion. "That's a tough one. I'm sorry, Ally. No joke."

"Me, too. Nick and I will spend some more time with him tomorrow then start for home."

"Already? So he said there's no place for Nick with him?"

"We haven't even broached that subject. There's no need to anymore. Things changed between Nick and me on this trip. He —" I hear the television come on inside the room. "I want him with me, Warren. I think I always did, I was just afraid of screwing everything up."

"I'm glad, honey. He's a nice kid."

"He is a nice kid. When he finally opened up to me, he made

me remember how it was to be his age. You may find this hard to believe, but there was a time when I was actually spontaneous. I'd forgotten that. I wasn't afraid of anything. Now —" I tap my fingernail against the phone. "Nick said you called me a workaholic."

"Tell him he has a big mouth."

"No, you were right. And I needed to hear it."

"So, what now?"

"He's going to come back with me. We'll figure out how to make it work as we go."

"I'm glad you two have made peace, but I don't want you to come home yet unless—"

"You don't—?"

"Just listen. When you come back, I want you to have all your questions answered. I won't compete with your past anymore, Ally. I want you to be sure where you belong."

A sudden gust of dry wind blows hair across my face. I start to protest again, to assure him I already know my place, that any doubts or questions I may have once had are already gone.

But I can't deny my need to reach out to Sonny. He's suffered as much as me; I know that now. There was a time in my life when I was so angry I told myself I'd misjudged his character, that he'd had his fill of me then walked away. Like Gary did with Sarah. Deep inside, though, I always knew it wasn't true.

There's a lot I still don't understand about the way we ended; I can't imagine any good excuse for the way in which he left. But, I know Sonny's a good man. I know he had his reasons. And, now, our losses bond us as surely as our love did.

As Warren and I say goodbye, the joy I felt today when Sonny looked at Nick and I saw his eyes soften, comes back to me. I remember watching them together, listening to the ease of their conversation. I remember the contentment of spending the day with them. The three of us like a family. The family I always imagined. Almost. Sonny and me and our grandson, instead of our daughter.

And I'm confused all over again.

CHAPTER 12

*W*e're at Sonny's by dawn the next morning. Yesterday, he explained that, though his cattle need little attention this time of year, every other day he rides out on horseback to count the herd and make sure none are sick. Nick wanted to go along. So we rose at an ungodly hour and drove out.

Since Nick is still not horse-ready, and he's almost as sore from yesterday's ride as I am, they take Sonny's pickup to the pasture. Afterward, they'll join his two hired hands, Ross and Clayton, who are preparing several empty sections of field to be planted with corn. I'm not sure what that entails. Though I'm interested, I decide Sonny and Nick could stand the time alone together without me.

I brought Sarah's journals with me. While Nick and Sonny are out, I go for a run then curl up on Sonny's sofa with Sly on the floor at my feet. Sipping coffee, I open a journal and read.

August 28, 1996

Dear Diary,

Nick started kindergarten today. Hurray! No more paying for child care. Still, I cried along with several of the other mothers when I left him in Mrs. Mehan's kindergarten classroom. We stood in the hallway, three of us, looking in at the kids, laughing and weeping at the same time. So silly, I know. But it seemed like the end of his babyhood, that he's that much closer to growing up and leaving me. He was scared, yet so brave. And so excited. We bought new sneakers, new jeans. He looked like such a big boy, and handsome as can be. The cutest boy in the room, if I do say so. And the smartest, too, I'm sure. He marched right up to the door, then broke my heart by dropping my hand and looking up at me with wide eyes. I understood that he wanted to act grown up when he went in, and that clinging to his mother would blow that image. I want so much for him. To do well. To make friends. To belong.

In other news, I went out with a friend of a friend of Carrie's last night. He was nice enough, but there wasn't a spark. Maybe I should stop expecting one. Or wanting one. Maybe nice enough is as good as it gets. In my limited experience, sparks tend to burn out, then fizzle, leaving you in the dark with nothing but ashes.

Off to bed now. Another day tomorrow of typing up divorce documents for others whose sparks have fizzled.

Later ~Sarah

I lose myself in entry after entry. Nick's first soccer game. Boy Scouts. A playground fight. His colds and earaches, a broken arm. His struggle with vocabulary words. Sarah's infatuation with Nick's middle-school football coach. Her broken heart when the man married someone else. Losing her job due to layoffs and having to move in with her parents. Her grief over the Pearsons' deaths in an automobile accident. Her uncertainty over how much to tell Nick about his father.

And then, I'm there, in the pages again, and so is Sonny.

June 16, 2001

Dear Diary,

I'm worried about Nick. He's become so quiet, so hard and distant. It started after he met Gary's parents. I tried for so long to shield him from the truth that his father is nothing but a loser. For a long time, he's had all these fantasies built up in his mind that Gary wanted to be with him but couldn't, for whatever reason. That all shattered when he met the Bowers. Then, when Mom and Dad died, he took it hard. Dad could be tough on him, but he was the only man in Nick's life. Now he's gone, too.

It makes me wonder about my birth father. Was he like Gary? Did he run off when he found out about me? Or did he even know I existed?

Since Mom and Dad died, I've been obsessing about the mystery parents. I found the adoption papers, and I've decided to try to locate them. The thought of meeting them terrifies me, but I need answers. And finding them won't hurt Mom and Dad anymore.

It's time.

~Sarah

I read through several more entries. Then I almost stop breathing.

January 8, 2003

Dear Diary,

The mystery mother's name is Allyson Cole. She lives in Portland. I did a search on the Internet and up popped an old article about the opening of her café years ago. Yesterday, Nancy and I drove there and, God, you should see her! She looks too young to be my mother. I found out through the adoption agency that she was only seventeen when I was born. Seventeen! No father was named, but of course, being that young, she wouldn't have been married.

Nancy kept urging me to talk to her, to tell her who I am, but I just couldn't. I tried. I went up to the buffet line when her help was busy with other things, but I ended up just asking for more bread.

She has a nice smile, olive skin, straight dark hair in a stylish cut that just touches her shoulders. Which tells me my coloring must come from the mystery father. So, now I guess I'll start cursing him for that legacy, instead of her. My own hair was a mess, but she still commented on it. She said it was beautiful, that her daughter's hair was the same shade, and then she looked at me in a way that made me think *she knows!* Oh, God! I thought I would faint.

But, of course she didn't know. That's silly. How would she recognize me? The article about her in the paper said that she is single and childless, so I assume I'm the daughter she mentioned, unless she gave up more than one red-haired baby girl. Wouldn't that be something? If I had a twin or an older or younger sister out there? Oh, great. Something else for me to obsess about. A mystery sister to go along with the mystery parents.

Anyway, it was so strange that we stood there looking at each other, so close I smelled the spicy scent of her perfume, two strangers linked by genetics and nothing else. Maybe that's why I couldn't speak up. When you get right down to it, we're strangers. That's it. But, I admit, my heart almost jumped out of my chest when she handed me the bread basket and our fingers brushed.

After seeing her, I don't know how I can ever approach her. She looks so, I don't know, polished, I guess. Like money. Nothing at all like me. Just the sight of her makes me feel less-than, you know? And then to read all she's accomplished. Obviously, she's a huge success, having her own business and everything. The place has even won awards.

I hate feeling so intimidated by her. And angry. What would she think of me? Would she be ashamed that I'm her daughter, at how little I've made of myself? I'm thirty-two years old and only a secretary with one year of college night school to my credit. The article said she got her graduate degree in business at twenty-four, then went on to culinary school. I guess all that was more important than me.

I can't stand feeling this bitter and insecure. I can't stand writing about her or thinking about her, but I can't stop, either.

~Sarah

I stare out the window. Sarah and I spoke. Our fingers touched. Why didn't I know? Why can't I remember?

Reaching for my bag, I put the journal inside, unable to suffer through another word. I feel I'm starting to know my daughter, to understand her heart. But I can only read so much at a time before the guilt overwhelms me. No wonder Nick directed so much anger toward me when we met. After reading his mother's thoughts, he knew how much pain I had caused her.

Suddenly, I yearn for Warren. The man knows how to listen and comfort and, right now, I need his shoulder, his arms around me. I remember Sarah's birthday last year. He made a big production to try to take my mind off things. He wanted to take me out for a fancy dinner then go to a jazz club. When he came to pick me up and found me red-eyed and still not close to ready, he took off his tie, made soup and tossed a salad. After we ate, he put on some music and rubbed my back while, for the first time, I poured out my soul to him, completely exposed the grief I felt over giving up my child.

I glance at my watch, see that it's close to noon. Sonny said they'd come home for lunch. I decide to look in his refrigerator and pantry and see if there's something I can whip up for him and Nick to eat.

After lunch, Sonny and I sit at the picnic table while Nick throws a Frisbee to Sly. A warm wind's hiss provides constant background noise to our conversation. It swirls dust devils along the dirt road leading to the house, whips hair across my face, grabs Nick's Frisbee and carries it off in the wrong direction, again and again. Sonny shows no sign of annoyance; I guess he's used to it.

I tuck a strand of hair behind my ear. "How did you end up in Mesquite Bend?" I ask him.

"A buddy of mine from 'Nam, Kent Bowman, grew up here. He came back to the States around the same time I did. After I got out of the hospital, he invited me to come spend some time with his family until I got back up to speed. It sounded more appealing than facing Mom and Roland out in Florida."

The mention of Roland, Sonny's stepdad, reminds me of his family situation. I never met his parents. They divorced when Sonny was very young. Afterward, his father dropped in and out of his life, then stopped showing up altogether. His mother married Roland and moved to Florida before Sonny graduated high school. He stayed behind in California, on his own.

After Sonny left me, I often wished I at least knew his mother's name so I could contact her to see if she knew where he was, what had happened to him. Other times, I felt so bitter and angry, I told myself I didn't want to know, that I wanted only to forget about him.

"So I came out here and stayed with the Bowmans, and I never left," Sonny finishes. "They put me to work at their feed store. Later, I filled in as a farmhand on the side. I don't know what I would've done without Kent and his family. They saved my sanity."

Shifting on the end of the bench, his leg stretched out, he

stares past Nick and Sly toward the pasture, memories I can't even imagine in his eyes.

I want to ask him more about that time in his life, about Vietnam, his recovery, but he acts closed off to it, now. Uncomfortable with the topic. Instead, I tell him what I've learned about Gary Bowers from Nick and through Sarah's journals. I also fill him in on what Nancy Pacheco told me about Nick's alcohol and marijuana possession charges, and about the pot I found in his bag.

"It's so awkward having to face these issues after not raising children. I've never had to think about this stuff, much less deal with it. And now, when I try to reason with Nick, I feel like..." I shake my head, push tangled, windblown hair from my face. "I don't know what I feel like."

"A hypocrite?" He chuckles. "I say that because we did the same things he is, and that's how I'm sure I'll feel if I have to address it with him.

Now, watching Nick laugh and tussle with Sly, it seems impossible that he's the same boy who stared at me through wasted, bleary eyes just days ago. "A hypocrite." I sigh. "That's exactly what I feel like. But, I can't just look the other way, you know? Sometimes, I hate being a grown-up."

Sonny chuckles again. "It sure puts a different perspective on things, doesn't it?"

"Yes, it does." I laugh, too. "At least my parents couldn't relate. Maybe that made it easier for them to lay down the law."

"How *is* your mom?" One corner of his mouth curves up. "And Professor Harold?"

"Bev says they're fine. They moved to Walla Walla a few years ago to be close to her. I don't talk to them much. Holidays and birthdays, but that's about it."

He doesn't ask why; he knew me well enough to guess the answer. "How is Bev? She was always a great girl."

"She's a great woman, too. She's been married to the same man for thirty-one years and they have two grown girls. She did a good job with them. She's a fabulous mother and a fabulous teacher. Everything you'd expect."

"Sounds to me like you have a pretty fabulous career yourself. And that you've done a good job with Nick so far, too."

"I hope so. For his sake and Sarah's. I owe her so much."

Sonny's mustache twitches, and he studies me with an intensity that makes me uncomfortable. I wish I hadn't been so open about my feelings concerning my obligation to our daughter's memory. I don't want him to ask about the comment. I want more time to process her last journal entry before I can talk about my guilt. Like a fresh cut, I need to keep it covered for a while.

"At least Nick hasn't mentioned wanting a cigarette since we've been here," I say, keeping the conversation on our grandson.

Sonny clears his throat. "I caught him smoking one earlier."

"Tell me you're kidding." I groan. "Where did he get it?"

"Who knows? Not from me. I quit a couple of years ago. Give him some time. You can't expect him to turn into a saint overnight. Or at all, for that matter." He chews on a toothpick and watches Nick. "What would you think about him staying with me, Al?"

"You mean permanently?"

"Sure. Why not? Small-town life would be good for him. Plus, I'd put him to work. He can help me harvest the wheat next month. I could use an extra hand. He could drive the grain cart while I drive the combine. We'll kill two birds with one stone. He'd help me save time, while I try to help him get his head straight. If nothing else, it'll keep him out of trouble."

I study Sonny as he shifts to watch Nick and the dog, a look of pure contentment on his face. "Is that the only reason you want him to stay?" I ask. "So you can help each other out?"

"He's all the family I have." Sonny glances at me and shrugs. "I'd like to get to know him better." He says it like it's no big deal, but what I glimpse in his eyes tells me otherwise. Loneliness. Caring. Need. Sonny needs someone in his life, someone to be close to, to lean on and care about, as much as Nick does.

It's what I wanted when Nick and I set out on this trip. For the two of them to hit it off, to be at ease with one another. For Sonny to want Nick to stay, and for Nick to be happy to do so. But now I'm filled with uncertainty. "We've just reached a place where we're comfortable together," I say quietly. "He's opening up to me. I'm not sure it's a good time to risk upsetting that."

"Give it some thought. What's he gonna do in Portland? You said he was already hanging out with that guy he met at your gym who's bad news."

"That was before this trip, when he was taking out his anger over Sarah's death on me."

"If he was here, it would free up your time. You could concentrate on planning your wedding to the guy who put that rock on your finger."

My hackles rise. "Is that what you think? That I don't have time for him, so I'm dropping him on you?"

"Whoa." Sonny holds up a hand. "I didn't mean to start an argument. I was just making a suggestion. Nick's welcome here for as long as he wants to stay. That's all I'm saying. I think we'd be good for each other. Think about it."

I'm not sure what irritates me more; Sonny's insinuation that Nick's an inconvenience for me, or the fact that he has no difficulty whatsoever integrating him into his life, when I find it so difficult to merge him into mine.

"Nick wants to live with me in Portland and that's what we're going to do." The obstinate sound of my voice embarrasses me.

"Why did you bring him here, Al? Just to meet me?"

Sonny could always see right through my stubbornness to the motive behind it. I don't think that's changed. Looking up, I watch Nick approach the table. "He's coming. We'll talk about this later."

When Nick sits down beside him at the picnic table, Sonny says, "Tonight's my bunko night."

"Bunko?" Nick says, scowling.

"Six couples meet once a month, and it's my turn to have it here this time. As it turns out, we're one couple short, so you two can fill in."

"What do you do?" I ask.

"It's a dice game, but it's really more of an excuse for my friends and me to get together and visit and have a good time. Everybody brings potluck for dinner, and sometimes we cut the game short and pull out the guitars for a little jam session."

"We don't want to intrude," I say, antsy at the prospect of meeting Sonny's friends.

"You won't be intruding. Like I said, we're one couple shy tonight. You'll save me the trouble of havin' to find alternates. And you can meet Kent. My buddy I told you about."

"I'm dying for a nap. I thought we'd go back to the motel for a while this afternoon."

"I'm not sleepy," Nick says. "Sonny's gonna give me another riding lesson."

"How can you even think about getting back on a horse this soon? I'm so sore I can hardly walk."

Laughing, Sonny picks up his hat and puts it on. "You go back to the motel if you want to, Al. Just be back by seven."

A look of worship crosses Nick's face when he looks at his grandfather, and I know I can't refuse. How am I supposed to compete against John Wayne for a teenage boy's affection? And why, all the sudden, do I feel as if I *must* compete? "You said it's potluck. What should I bring?"

One side of Sonny's mouth curves up. "Just yourself."

When Sonny said "couples," it didn't occur to me that he had a female counterpart. I don't know why I didn't assume he would. He's still good-looking. Only now, ruggedly so, with his twinkling green eyes that seem to pierce right through me, and that silver-gray hair and masculine work-hardened body.

Her name is Cindy Cobly, and she's in her late forties. Short, curvy and bottle-blond, she has a thick Texas twang and eyes that shoot daggers at me.

All through dinner, she's quiet, watching me and listening while the others ask questions. Sonny's frank, as always, but doesn't offer more information than necessary. I guess he figures there's no need for pretense, since Nick already knows the truth.

With twelve of us crowded around a kitchen table filled with barbecued beef, potato salad, coleslaw and assorted desserts, he says I was his girl way back in the sixties when we were just kids, and that Nick's our grandson and we're out for a visit.

A hush blankets the room.

"Well, what'd'ya know?" Kent Bowman finally says, breaking the silence.

I liked Sonny's war buddy the moment I met him. Kent is bald, broad-shouldered and stocky, with a beer belly and a constant smile. It's easy to imagine him taking in a hurting friend, making Sonny a part of his family.

After considering me for a time, Kent shifts to Sonny then back to me again. "So you're Al. I didn't make the connection when we met earlier." My hand rests on the table next to his. He covers it with his palm and squeezes my fingers. "I've heard a lot about you."

We recognize each other. I'm a missing piece of Kent's puzzle; he's a missing piece of mine. Found unexpectedly. We each have answers to the others' questions. Questions about Sonny. A man we both care about.

But now's not the time.

I smile at him while trying to pretend I'm not bothered by all the watchful eyes aimed my direction. Nobody dares ask about mine and Sonny's relationship, though it's obvious they want to.

While the men set up three card tables in the living room for the bunko game, drink beer and shoot the breeze, the women clean up the kitchen in true non-feminist fashion. When the trash is full, I take the bag outside to a metal can I noticed earlier at the side of the house. As I start back in, Cindy corners me on the porch.

"You enjoying your visit?" She sets an ashtray on the porch railing then leans back against the railing and lights a cigarette.

"Yes, I am."

"How long you stayin'?"

"I don't know. Not long."

"You're the girl in the picture, aren't you?"

"Picture?"

"The one in Sonny's bedroom. On his nightstand."

Surely not, I think. After thirty-six years, he wouldn't still have my photograph next to his bed. "I don't know. I haven't seen it."

She looks relieved to hear that I haven't been near Sonny's bed. "The girl he left behind when he went to 'Nam in sixty-nine?"

I nod, the pace of my heartbeat picking up. I didn't know he left that soon.

"He didn't tell me you had a child together."

"He didn't know."

I recognize the surprise in her expression as she takes a drag off the cigarette then blows out a long stream of smoke. "Sonny's a good man. He's been through a lot. I'd hate to see him get hurt again."

"I'm not here to hurt him, Cindy." Behind her hard edge of jealousy, I see the same softness I heard in her voice when she spoke his name. "And I'm not here to threaten you, either. Whatever's between you and Sonny—"

"It's not serious between us. Not yet."

I bite back a smile. Serious enough that she knows what's on his bedroom nightstand.

Blinking, she looks away, embarrassed. "Sonny's gun-shy after two failed marriages. He deserves to be happy."

Now I'm the one surprised. Sonny didn't tell me about any marriages.

"Maybe he fit in the city back when you knew him, but I

doubt he would now," Cindy continues. "And you don't look like you'd last much more than a week out here."

I start to defend myself then realize two things: Cindy Cobly loves Sonny, and she's right about both of us. I laugh. "I wouldn't even want to try."

Her shoulders relax, and she finally smiles at me. "Okay then." She picks up the ashtray, crushes her cigarette into it, nodding at the door. "You ready to play?"

"Let's go."

Nick and I are partners in the dice game. It's all about luck, not skill, and is easy to learn. Sonny and his friends are fun and rowdy. After about an hour, we take a break. Sonny brings out the tequila, limes and shot glasses. I gather it's a monthly ritual considering the stories of other bunko nights they share.

"None for me," I say with a laugh, backing away from the kitchen counter when Sonny places a shot glass in front of me.

He smiles his crooked smile. "Ah, come on, Al. For old times' sake. Giving up red meat's bad enough, don't tell me you gave up drinking, too? You didn't even have a beer."

"I pretty much stick to wine these days."

"That's a relief. I'd hate to hear you've turned into one of those boring, holier-than-thou people with no vices at all."

He tilts both the bottle and his head in my direction. "What do you say?"

"Okay, just one. More than that and I'd be dancing on the card tables. You wouldn't want that."

Sonny's brow cocks in a way that sends my pulse through the roof. "Don't be so sure about that."

Everyone laughs. Except Cindy, that is. I feel her stare from across the kitchen. Nick's, too. Both of them analyzing how Sonny and I are together. Each for different reasons.

"Hey," Nick complains, when everyone has their shot ready. "You forgot me."

"Nice try, kid." Sonny slaps his back. "Maybe in five years we'll share one, what'd'ya say?"

"I say that stinks." He frowns and crosses his arms, making everyone laugh again.

Sonny lifts his glass. "You've gotta be sober to drive your grandma home later after she dances on the card tables." He nods at the group. *"Salud."*

The group echoes the toast. Everyone bites into a salted lime wedge and the tequila goes down.

Sonny's gaze meets mine as the heat spreads through my chest. His eyes burn like the liquor. I recognize that green fire and know what it means. Looking away, I tell myself he's had too much to drink, that's all. That's why I've caught him watching me all night. Even as a kid, he always got silly and sentimental when he drank too much. And got ideas.

We never resume the bunko game. More shots go around for the men and a woman named Kay; the rest of us refrain.

I like the easy camaraderie between Sonny and his friends. He and Kent, especially. It's easy to see how close they are, how familiar with one another.

"I hope you hold your liquor better than last time, Son." Kent clicks his glass against Sonny's. "Any hittin' on my wife tonight and you and me are gonna go 'round and 'round."

Jan, Kent's wife, laughs and rolls her eyes toward Cindy. "Here they go."

Sonny winks at Jan. "As I recall, she was the one flirtin' with me. Can I help it if you're not man enough to keep her satisfied, Kenny boy?"

The teasing banter continues as they build a fire outside in a pit behind the house. Lawn chairs are hauled out, along with a cooler of iced-down beer.

Sonny brings two guitars from the house, one for him and one for Kent. I hug myself against the chill in the air and stare into the flames as they play. Cindy sings in a voice so clear and emotional it brings tears to my eyes. It's a stereotypical country song about being away from the one you love. It makes me think of Warren, and I wish he was here to watch the fire with me, to wrap his arms around me and sway to the music.

When I glance up, Cindy's watching Sonny as she sings, and he's watching me. I'm not the only one who notices. The other three women in the group, Cindy's friends, exchange raised-brow glances.

When the song ends, Sonny finishes off his beer and reaches into the cooler for another. He must sense the tension, because he changes the pace of things by starting to play an old, upbeat rock tune, "Brown Eyed Girl." This time, he sings and strums and picks, while everyone claps along.

He used to practice his guitar all the time when I knew him, but he wasn't this good back then. Still, I've missed hearing his tenor voice, the music his hands make.

Under a pearl moon, with the orange fire crackling and music floating in the air, I can't help thinking again of Woodstock and our last night together. I still don't have any concrete answers about why he left the next morning, though I have my suspicions now that I know he went to Vietnam. Since arriving in Mesquite Bend, Nick's always been close by, and the time never feels right to pursue the subject.

Or maybe that's only an excuse; maybe I'm just afraid to hear the truth after all this time. What if all the resentment I held on to for so long was as unjustified as it's beginning to seem? But that's what I'd hoped for, wasn't it? Did he know at Woodstock that he'd been drafted? Was he trying to keep me from waiting for him? Agonizing that he wouldn't make it home alive? All noble motives, but he didn't save me from agonizing. I still did, but for different reasons. I deserved the truth, deserved to be there for him.

Only ice floats in the cooler by the time Sonny stops playing. He and Kent and the other two men talk and laugh too loud, telling jokes that only *they* find funny. They douse the fire and we carry the lawn chairs inside.

Cindy's no good at hiding her feelings. She tries to prolong leaving, but since she rode out with Kent and Jan, she has no choice but to go when they do.

Sonny shakes all the men's hands, hugs all the women, giving Cindy an added peck on the cheek before she climbs into the backseat of Kent's old Jeep Cherokee. As she reaches to close her door, I say, "We'd better be going, too, Sonny." I want her to know that I don't have any desire to overthrow her romantic plans.

Sleepy-eyed, he glances back at me. "Don't go yet. I have some business with Nick first."

"Be careful," I say to the designated drivers.

Sonny waves and bellows, "I love you guys."

I bite my lip to keep from laughing.

As the two vehicles drive away, we stand in the yard, watching until their taillights shrink into tiny, twin red dots in the darkness, then disappear.

Sonny squints up at the moon. "Would you look at that? Come here, you two."

We join him in the center of the yard. Even Sly, who has

been timid around the crowd, stirs and comes down off the porch.

Sonny leans toward Nick and says in a slurred half whisper, "I bet'cha we could call up some coyotes. Wanna give it a try?"

He staggers on his bad leg, and Nick grabs hold of his grandfather's arm and laughs. "Sure. How?"

Throwing back his head, Sonny howls, sending Sly into a barking frenzy. "Shhhhh." He holds a finger to his lips. "Quiet, dog." He waits until Sly settles down then says, "Listen."

We all lean forward, straining to hear an echoing answer. Only crickets respond. After half a minute, Sonny says, "You try, Nick."

Nick tilts his head back, but only bursts out laughing, making me laugh, too.

"Hey, now." Sonny scowls at us. "This is serious business. Come on, kid."

Nick tries again, doubles over, and then pulls himself together. Straightening, he lets loose a convincing rendition of a coyote call. When he finishes, I grab Sly to calm him and we all listen again. The only sound, besides crickets, is the whinny of a horse in the barn.

Sonny grins at me. "You give 'er a go, Al."

"I can't howl."

"Don't get all prissy on us. Sure you can. I know you better than that."

Shaking my head, I take a deep breath and try to imitate him and Nick.

Sonny crosses his arms and makes a face at me. "That has to be the puniest, most pathetic half-ass attempt at a howl I ever heard."

I lift my chin. "I beg your pardon."

He turns to Nick. "Am I right?"

Nick laughs. "It was a girl-howl, all right."

"Oh, really?" I lift a brow. "Then what's that I hear?"

We get very quiet. In the distance, a coyote answers my call.

"That's awesome!" Nick shrieks.

Hooting, Sonny pulls off his hat and throws it skyward. *"All right, Al."* With a lopsided grin, he lifts his fists, beats on his chest and bellows like Tarzan, then staggers backward. His bad leg goes out from under him. Nick catches him before he falls. *"Whoa, now."*

Nick looks across at me. "I think he's drunk."

"No kidding." I scoop Sonny's hat off the ground and take hold of his other arm. "Don't you have cattle to check in the morning?"

"Bright and early," Sonny answers with another sloppy grin, then starts singing "Brown Eyed Girl" again at the top of his lungs.

"We'd better get him to bed, Nick." I wrap an arm around him. "Go open the door. I can get him up the steps."

"...sha-la-la-la-la-la-la-la-la-la-la-ti-da," Sonny shrieks. When Nick is out of earshot, he stops singing, turns his mouth to my ear and says in a low voice, "Why don't *you* just take me to bed, Al? Mmm...I might just have to eat you up, you smell so good." He nips my lobe.

"And you smell like a brewery," I hiss, experiencing déjà vu. I think I've heard those same words from him a long time ago. "Shhh." His mustache tickles my neck. I look up at Nick. He's holding the door and doesn't appear to have heard. "Sonny McGraw, you're going to have a headache the size of Texas in the morning."

When we pass through the doorway, Nick takes Sonny's

other arm. "We should stay the night so we can make sure he gets up in the morning."

"Something tells me this isn't the first time he's gone to bed wasted on bunko night." I stagger, pause and shift Sonny's weight. "He's done fine without us before."

Sonny moans. His head rolls back on his shoulders.

"I'm staying," Nick says.

We drop Sonny facedown on his bed. He's snoring before the mattress stops squeaking.

I toss his hat beside him, look at the clock on the nightstand, see that it's almost midnight. Then I'm startled by the sight of the photograph Cindy mentioned. It sits in a frame beside the clock. The same photograph I have at home, the one of us together, me wearing the blue peasant blouse, the flower in my hair, the yellow beads.

With a snort, Sonny resumes snoring. I smile and close my eyes. I'd rather not drive into town this late alone. "Okay," I say to Nick. "I'll sleep in the other bedroom, you take the couch."

I grab hold of the boot on Sonny's good leg and tug until it comes off. Hesitating, I reach for the other one. I don't know what to expect; considering my roller-coaster emotions lately, I'm not sure I can handle whatever's beneath that boot without falling apart.

"Maybe we should leave it on," Nick whispers. "He might not want you to see."

"Good point." Relieved, I pull the edge of the bedspread up and over Sonny.

"He showed it to me, though. It was cool."

I make a face. *"Nick."*

"I mean, it would suck to lose a leg, but the fake one is pretty awesome in a way."

"Did you ask to see it, or did he volunteer?"

"I asked." When I widen my eyes, Nick says, "He was okay with it. He said he'd rather have his real one, but that you've got to look at the bright side."

"There's a bright side?"

"He said it's five less toenails to clip."

I look at Sonny, snoring into the pillow, one boot on, one off, and I don't know whether to laugh or cry.

So, after I go to bed, I do a little of both.

CHAPTER 13

The front door's squeak wakes me the next morning. I hear Nick's laughter and Sonny's voice. Scooting to the edge of the bed, I push aside the curtain and look out the window. They're climbing into Sonny's truck. One of those famous West Texas sunrises he bragged about blushes on the horizon.

I stashed a pair of running shoes in my car trunk, along with jeans and a T-shirt; I brought the change of clothes knowing, with Sonny in charge, we might end up on a horse or a hike or whatever activity popped into his mind on impulse.

Jogging along the dirt road that stretches across Sonny's leased property, I begin to understand better what drew him to this desolate land. The morning sky opens before me, offering no obstacles to block my way. I feel like I could run right up to the blended layers of pink and purple and royal blue and climb them, one by one, until I reach the orange sun above.

After the war, did Sonny need a place without boundaries? An uncomplicated place so open in every direction he could lose himself in the emptiness? Where he could see clearly what lay ahead, as well as behind him?

When I return to the house, I take a quick shower and put on the same sundress I wore last night. I decide to straighten some of the leftover clutter from the bunko party before driving back to town to change and put on makeup. It's starting to feel ridiculous, my being here in Mesquite Bend, interrupting Sonny's routine. The town's so small there's nothing for me to do to fill my day. Soon, we'll have to get things out in the open, settle the past, for my sake, if not his. Then Nick and I will go home.

I'm one-hundred-percent sure Nick won't want to leave. I've never seen him so happy. He's a kid here, not bitter and jaded beyond his years like he was when he arrived on my doorstep. Still, we have to get on with our life together. I can't imagine, can't bear the thought, of going back without him. Not anymore. I love my work and Warren, but now that's not enough. Nick's a part of me, too.

Ready to leave, I gather my purse and the clothes I ran in when I hear a vehicle pull into the driveway. A door slams. Because of his prosthesis, the sound of Sonny's gait on the porch is distinctive.

He comes into the house alone. "Hey, Al. You're up."

"What's even more surprising is that *you* are." I smile. "How's your head?"

"I've had years of experience with hangovers. I'm surviving."

"Where's Nick?"

"Out plowing with Ross and Clayton. He wanted to try his luck driving the tractor."

"Is that safe?"

"Ross won't leave his side. He won't let him get in any

trouble." He nods at the door. "I thought we'd take a walk. We haven't had much of a chance to talk alone."

I clasp my hands behind me as we stroll through the grass toward a grove of shady cottonwood trees. The sky is clear blue now. The sun warms my face.

Sonny clears his throat. "I should probably apologize for anything I might've said to you last night that was out of line."

"You don't remember?"

"Not completely."

"Then what makes you think you said anything out of line?"

"I do remember some things." Scratching his chin, he slants me a sheepish, lopsided smile. "Like what the sight of you in that dress did to me."

"Oh." I glance down, flattered and uneasy at the same time. "Maybe I should go change. Just so you don't get any ideas," I tease.

"Too late." His cheek twitches. "But I promise I'll be good." He takes my left hand and glances down at my ring. "If you weren't wearing this, I wouldn't make that promise."

I'm stunned that, at my age, he can still make me blush.

"Tell me about him, Al."

We link fingers. I look down at the ground. "His name's Warren Noble. He's a surgeon and a really great guy. He's the only man I've ever said 'yes' to." I feel Sonny's stare and, when I glance up, two amused and doubtful green eyes greet me. Punching his arm, I say, "To marriage, wise guy. I said 'yes' to marriage."

"You never married?"

I shake my head.

"A woman like you?" He stops walking, faces me, frowning. "Why?"

"I wish I had an easy answer to that. I'm not sure myself why I never let anyone else get close." I swallow my nervousness. "I've had a hard time letting go of the past."

He tightens his grip on my fingers. "I'm sorry."

The old emotions stir in me, and I know I'm still not ready to hear what happened to him, why he made the decision he did to leave me. Not yet. I'm not sure the time will ever be right. Maybe I've already had all I can handle. Nick showing up, learning about Sarah's death and the loss of Sonny's leg in Vietnam.

"It's okay now," I say quickly. "Warren broke through all that. He stuck by me through a year of complete stubbornness."

I recall Warren's frustration, at times. The night, months ago, when he said, "Enough." A week of me tying up the phone lines to Bev, crying in her ear, her crooning soothing words to me one minute and telling me what a fool I was the next. Then Warren ringing my doorbell, at last, just after dawn on a cold, rainy morning, his arms full of fresh mint, rosemary and red lettuce he found at a market that opened early, saying he would've brought roses, but no florist was open that time of day. It didn't matter. To me, what he brought meant more than roses ever could.

"Like I said, he's a wonderful man," I say quietly, touched again by the memory. "I don't deserve him."

"Sure you do. You deserve the best man there is, Al. You love him?"

"Yes." I nod. "I do."

"I'm happy for you then. That's good."

We start off for the trees again. "No, you're wrong. I don't deserve Warren. Because, the truth is, I'm still not sure. Oh, I'm sure about *him*, just not about marriage. It scares me, the whole commitment thing."

"Sounds like you're already committed, marriage or not. A year and a half is a long time to be with someone."

"Not really," I say, his comment making me wonder about his romantic relationships.

He shrugs but doesn't offer any information to satisfy my curiosity.

"Even though Warren would never do anything to hurt me, even though I know he loves me and wants to be with me, I can't stop imagining that some morning I'll wake up and—" My heart collides against my chest when I stop myself from saying more.

"Al…"

Sonny slows his step, but I keep up my pace until I'm a few feet ahead of him. I turn to face him, then walk slowly backward. "What about you?" Cocking my head, I decide to ask about his love life, whether it's my business or not. "Cindy Cobly said you've been married before."

"Twice married. Twice divorced." He catches up to me and grabs my arm. "Better watch where you're going. You almost stepped in a prairie-dog hole."

I turn around and walk alongside him. "How long did the marriages last?"

"Not more than a year each time." Which explains his earlier comment about the length of my relationship with Warren.

"Did you love your wives?" I ask, and he looks across at me quickly.

"You don't beat around the bush, do you, Al?"

"You just asked me the same question about Warren."

"So I did."

"Well, did you?"

He holds my gaze. "I tried to love them. But they weren't you."

Surprised and flustered, I clasp my hands behind my back as we walk and search his face, remembering the framed photo on his nightstand. "Sonny...I..." Touched, stunned and saddened all at once, I clear my throat, shifting my gaze away from him then back again. "What's going on between you and Cindy Cobly?"

"We're just friends."

I give him a skeptical grin. "Wake up, cowboy. Don't you see how she looks at you? She wanted to scratch my eyes out last night."

Sonny waves me off. "We've been keeping each other company for the last year or so, since her divorce. I've already screwed up two marriages; I'm not looking to try again. Cindy knows that."

"Maybe so. But, trust me, she's going to do her best to change your mind."

His huff suggests that I'm talking nonsense. "What about Nick?" he says, maneuvering the subject as deftly as I did. "Have you given any more thought to him staying with me?"

"I think Portland would be an easier transition for him. He'll be close to Seattle and his old friends. They could visit or he could go there from time to time."

"Al, that doesn't make sense."

The statement catches me off guard, jars me. When we reach the trees, he leans against one, I lean against another, my pulse thumping unsteadily.

"He was headed for trouble in Seattle," Sonny continues. "Hell, he was already in trouble. Don't you think he needs to leave all that behind? Including the friends that were more than likely doing the same things he was?"

A part of me knows he's right. Another part doesn't want to admit it. "All his things are in Portland and Seattle. I still haven't moved him out of the Pachecos' house. You're welcome to visit him any time, Sonny. And he can visit you."

"Like one of his friends." His expression is as cold as his voice. "Maybe I want more than that."

"Maybe I want more than a long-distance relationship with him, too." Tension knots in my stomach. "I'm not willing to move to Mesquite Bend. Are you willing to move to Portland?"

"Nick needs a man's influence. I know what I'm talking about. If my dad had been around for me, I think I would've had an easier time growing up."

"He'll have Warren."

"Not ten minutes ago you said you weren't sure about the guy."

"No, I didn't." It's as if he's manipulating my words, cornering me, pressuring me to make a decision I'm not comfortable making. "I *said* I wasn't sure about marriage."

"You think the guy's gonna have anything to do with Nick if you don't marry him? Besides, he's not Nick's flesh and blood."

"The Pearsons weren't Sarah's flesh and blood, either, Sonny." I blink back tears. "I wasn't there for our daughter. Because of a decision I made when I was a mixed-up kid, I didn't get to know her. I missed everything, Sonny. Everything. It's too late for her, but not for Nick. I'm going to know his friends, go to his graduation, help him through college."

He pushes away from the tree and crosses the space separating us. "So pacifying *your* guilt over Sarah by having

Nick live with you is more important than doing what's best for *him*. Is that what you're saying, Al?"

My frayed self-control snaps like a rotted rope, unleashing more than three decades of bitterness. Digging my fingers into my palms to keep from slapping his face, I ask, "What makes you so sure you're what's best for Nick? And how dare you judge me, Sonny? You weren't there to help me stand up to my parents. You weren't there to help me make the toughest decision of my life. You weren't there when I had to walk away from our baby." Shaking, I turn and stare at the house with my back to us, determined not to cry. "You weren't there, Sonny."

The silence stretches, then, "Al...I'm sorry. I shouldn't have said that." He sounds devastated. Right now, I hope he is. "I'm not handling this right."

I refuse to face him. I feel as miserable as he sounds.

"Look at me, Al."

"If I do, I'll hit you."

"Hit me, then."

I watch a truck turn onto the road leading to his house. "You have company."

"It's Clayton." A frustrated breath rushes out of him. "I better go see if something's wrong. Wait here. I'll be back."

"No." I start toward the house, still not making eye contact with him. "You have a farm to run. Nick can spend the day with you if he wants. I'm going to drive into Amarillo to do some shopping."

On the way to town, I call Teena, then Warren. "I miss your face," I say in greeting when he answers.

"I'm glad to hear that. I miss yours, too."

"And your arms, and your lips and your great big—"

"If you say 'heart' I'm going to be very disappointed." Warren chuckles.

"Well, I do miss your heart, but that's not what I was going to say." I sigh. "How are things there?"

"Busy, but good."

Desperate to take my mind off Nick and Sonny, if only for a few minutes, I ask, "So what do you think about this thing between Reid and Teena?"

"Reid and Teena? *My* Reid and *your* Teena? Teena of the purple hair and pierced tongue?"

"Reid didn't like how the tongue felt when he kissed her, so she took it out. You didn't know about all this?"

"No, I didn't—" He blurts a laugh. "I hope Marjorie has plenty of Valium on hand. Knowing her, she'll need it."

I smile. "I'm ready to come home."

"Are you sure?" I hear hope in his voice.

"Yes, I'm totally sure." Though, deep down I know it's mostly because, right now, I'm angry at Sonny.

"So, you and McGraw talked about what happened?"

"Well, no. Not really."

Silence, then, "Okay. Good. Come home."

"What's wrong?"

"Nothing's wrong. I just miss you."

A tumbleweed dances across the highway ahead of me. "I'll be there before you know it. I love you."

"I love you, too."

We talk awhile longer about travel plans then end the call.

Less than a minute later, my cell phone rings.

"Ally." Warren's sigh is heavy. "I want you to come home, you know I do. I never wanted you to go there in the first place. But I've been talking to Bev while you've been away and—"

"Oh, boy. What—?"

"She says you're not going to put the past away and move on until all that with McGraw is out in the open. Until you know the whole story, good or bad."

"Maybe it's better left untold. I don't want to get into it with him, Warren. The man can be a real son of a bitch." I know I'm exaggerating out of anger and feel bad the second I call Sonny something he's absolutely not, but I don't correct myself, for Warren's sake.

"Son of a bitch or not," Warren says, "I think Bev's right. What he did has tortured you for thirty-six years and kept you from marrying me."

I blow a noisy breath into the phone. "Okay, we'll talk. But day after tomorrow, no matter what, Nick and I are out of here. If I have to look at one more cow or one more stalk of wheat any time soon I think I'll scream. And, God, I'm hungry. All we've had to eat since I've been here is beef, beef and more beef."

"You're eating *red meat?"*

"It's either that or a steady diet of baked beans and potato salad."

"Well, it's only been a couple of days." He chuckles. "It *is* cattle country. The man's a rancher. What did you expect?"

"I asked him about the nearest place to eat seafood and he told me there's someplace called the Catfish Dock forty miles from here. *Catfish.* When's the last time you saw one of those in the ocean? Sonny grew up in California, but you'd never know it now. He's Texan through and through."

"I'll take you out for lobster when you get home."

"Stop it, you're making me drool."

"Or shrimp etouffee."

"Enough! I can't stand it." My cell phone crackles.

"You're fading out on me," Warren says. "I need to get to the hospital, anyway. I'll call you tonight."

"Okay."

"Promise you'll talk to him before you leave, all right? Get everything out in the open, like Bev says."

Everything out in the open. No more imagined scenarios. Decades of wondering finally over. Dread sweeps through me. Why does my sister have to be so right? "I will. I promise," I say.

Nick calls in the middle of my shopping spree to say he wants me to pick him up when I get back. He'll stay with me tonight at the motel. That's a surprise. Earlier, he gave me the impression he wanted to stay at Sonny's again. I'm afraid to ask what changed his mind.

Later that night, after Warren and I talk and Nick settles in for a little television, I talk to Teena.

"Everything all right?" Nick asks, when I hang up.

"Everything's fine," I answer. Almost too fine, in fact. Things at the café are running quiet smoothly without me. "Teena says hello."

"What's Warren been doing?"

"Working, mostly."

"He hasn't been to the river without me, has he?"

I smile. "He didn't mention it."

"Good." Nick picks up the remote and flips the channel.

"Is everything okay with you and Sonny, Nick?"

He shrugs. "Yeah."

"I'm surprised you didn't want to spend the night with him again."

"I thought you might want some company."

"That's nice of you." And I don't believe it for a minute.

Again, he flips the channel. "Sonny said he'd teach me how to move the cattle when I'm better at riding a horse."

"Really?"

"Yeah, and he said if I keep practicing roping the dummy steer, he has this friend who can teach me to head and heel."

"What's that?"

"Like they do in rodeos. There are two riders, one ropes the cow and the other ties it up."

"Sounds dangerous."

"Sonny said not if you know what you're doing."

So...*Sonny said*, did he? I reach to the nightstand for my bottle of hand lotion, take off my ring, pump three squirts into my hand. I know what Sonny McGraw is up to. Like Bev said, I tried to win Nick over with a computer and video-game equipment. Sonny's using horses and cattle and rodeos. Only *he's* trying to win Nick from *me*. And it's starting to look as if he's succeeding. I rub the lotion briskly up and down my arms.

"He's gonna buy me a pair of boots that'll be better for me to ride in."

"Is that right?"

"Yeah, and maybe even my own horse."

I take a deep breath. "Is there something you want to ask me, Nick?"

He turns to stare at the television, his face splotchy red all of a sudden. "Nope."

"You sure? Because there's nothing we can't talk about." Like the fact that living with his grandfather is starting to sound good to him. That's what this is all about. I should tell him it's okay, if that's what he wants. He shouldn't be afraid to admit he has changed his mind. But I can't bring myself to speak the words.

Irritated at both Sonny and myself, I slide my ring back on.

"So, when are you and Warren getting married?" Nick nods at the ring. "I saw him give you that before we left."

I fluff my pillow, prop it behind me, pull it out and fluff it again. "I'm not sure. I have some things to work out first."

"With Sonny?"

I slant him a look. "You don't beat around the bush, do you, Nick?"

He grins. "That sounds like something Sonny would say."

"Maybe because that's where I heard the expression."

"Did you love him back when you two knew each other?"

"Yes."

"Do you still?"

Considering how to answer that, I cross my arms. "He was my first love." I smile as the warmth of old memories eases my frustration. "We had a child together. Your mom. For those reasons, part of me will always love him. But we're different people now. We have very different lives and want different things." With the exception of one thing. Nick. We both want him. "I still love the part of Sonny that will always be the eighteen-year-old boy I knew."

It's a good answer, I think. The right answer. The only one that makes sense.

"But you also love Warren."

I nod. "Very much."

"He's cool."

"I'm glad you think so because you two are going to be spending a lot of time together."

Nick flips the channel again and looks away from me. "Sonny's cool, too."

"Yes, I guess he is."

After cruising through every channel and starting over, Nick says, "You think a person can love two people at once?"

"If you're asking if I think it's possible for you to care equally for Sonny and Warren, yes, I do. You have a lot of love in you. Plenty to go around."

"I'm not talking about that. I mean, to be *in* love with two people."

"Wow, Nick. That's quite a question. Do you have a couple of girls in mind you can't choose between?"

He makes a face. "Not me. *You.*"

Right now, I think I liked it better when he wouldn't talk to me. "Hmm. Maybe it's possible for a woman to love two men, but I'm not sure about the *in love* thing." I hesitate a second, then ask, "Why?"

He shrugs. "I was just wondering."

And now, thanks to Nick, I'm wondering, too.

CHAPTER 14

*O*ur last day. When I tell Nick we're leaving tomorrow, he balks, as I suspected he would.

"Already? We spent more time on the road than here."

We're on our way to Sonny's house. I called him earlier this morning and, when I told him we'd be going home tomorrow, he insisted on taking the day off and leaving the farm with Ross and Clayton. "Sonny has a business to run. So do I, Nick."

"But—" His jaw muscle jumps when I glance across at him. His foot taps the floorboard. "Have you asked him—" He stops abruptly and turns away.

"Did I ask him what?"

"Nothing."

"What?"

"It's no big deal. Never mind."

I don't need an answer to know what he's wondering. I was right last night. He's changed his mind; he wants to stay here. Is he afraid he'll hurt my feelings if he says it? Not that they wouldn't be hurt, but that's my problem, not Nick's. "You can talk to me, Nick. Whatever's on your mind, I won't get mad."

"Nothing's on my mind."

At Sonny's house, we load an empty ice chest and Sly into the bed of his truck, pile into the front then go to the grocery store. This time, I choose the food.

The drive to Palo Duro Canyon State Park offers no surprises in scenery. That is, until we're close and, suddenly, the ground opens up. It's as if Mother Nature pressed a knife blade into the flat, colorless land, cut out a huge, jagged bowl then painted it in deep, rich shades of orange, gold and sienna.

We park at a campsite then hike along a muddy creek that slithers like a red snake through the canyon floor. Following a trail, we climb to a series of small caves we look into, but don't risk entering. Nick's in heaven as we hike. So is Sly. He'll need extra shampoo when we bathe him tonight.

At noon, we picnic on tuna sandwiches, carrot sticks and fruit instead of deli meat and potato chips. Nick and Sonny tease me about the "girlie meal," but don't complain too much. They eat every bite.

Yesterday's argument still hangs in the air between Sonny and me. The anger is gone, but we're cautious with one another, ridiculously polite. I don't want to spoil the day, so I try not to think too much about how or when I'll bring up the question we've dodged since I arrived.

After lunch, we wash up and change into clean clothes at the park's facilities. There's even a place to give Sly a good scrub. Then we drive to Amarillo where we ride go-karts and have dinner at a restaurant Sonny promises will prove "you can get decent seafood" in this landlocked part of the country. He's right. The grilled tuna steak is decent. Or maybe I'm just starved for it.

When we arrive back at Sonny's that night, the three of us

settle in to watch a movie, a comedy Nick rented on the way home. But the action-packed day catches up to him, and he and Sly quickly doze off.

Sonny covers Nick with a blanket on the sofa and turns off the lamp. "You interested in finishing this?" He gestures at the television.

"Not really."

He leads me into the kitchen where we close the door so as not to wake Nick.

"You want me to make coffee?" he asks as I sit at the table.

"No, I'm fine." I don't need caffeine; my nerves are already on edge.

Sonny sits across from me. "Al, I'm sick about what I said yesterday. It didn't come out right. I've never been great with words, you know that." When I don't answer, he clears his throat. "But I still believe the best place for Nick is here with me. I'm not just saying that for selfish reasons. Though I admit I'd love having him here."

I lean back, cross my arms. "But you still think I *am* being selfish for wanting him with me."

"I'm sure you want what's best for him, too. We just don't agree on what that is."

"Nick hasn't ever lived in a home with two parents. Warren and I can give him that."

He tilts his head to one side and squints at me. "But you said you're not even sure about marrying the guy."

That again. I promised myself this conversation wouldn't evolve into another argument, but already he has me on the defensive. "What did you do, Sonny? Memorize every little thing I've said to you since we arrived so you could use it against me? You'll do or say anything to get your way, won't you?"

"And you'll argue with me until you wear me out and I give up. Even though you know good and well I'm right about this."

"You always did think you were right about everything."

"And you always were as hardheaded as your dad, even though you bitched about him."

A memory hits me, and when his eyes become tender, I know it hit him, too. We've made the same accusations to one another before, said almost the identical words. So long ago. During another disagreement. In the tent at Woodstock when he insisted we leave, and I wasn't ready. He made every argument for going, from the rain and mud, to the lack of food, to the drug-laced Kool-Aid. I wonder now if our lives would've taken a different turn if I'd given in.

Sonny grins. So do I.

He smooths his mustache. "Jesus. Listen to us. Butting heads, just like old times."

I reach across the table, and he takes my hand.

"Stay here for a second," he says. "I have something to show you."

He leaves for a minute and returns carrying a shoe box. Sitting in the chair next to mine, he takes off the lid. Faded photographs fill the box. Photographs of us and our friends and Bev, all taken during the six months Sonny and I dated.

"Look at us," I say, and we both laugh. "God, were we ever really that young? I have some of these same pictures. I took them out the other night before we left Portland to come here. When I looked at myself, it was almost like I was looking at someone else. A girl I barely remember."

Sonny touches my image on the photo he holds. "I remember. I remember everything about you back then."

His tender expression tugs at my heart, making me so aware of how our lives are woven together. "I do, too. Now. Oh, there are plenty of things I never forgot." *The way I felt about you. The dreams I had for the two of us.* "But Nick brought the rest of it back to me. I'd forgotten how insecure I was about my own strength, and how fearless about the things that I realize now should've scared me to death."

"Like running all over the country with a wild, red-haired kid who had more nerve than good sense?"

I smile. "Something like that."

Sonny returns his attention to the photo. After a while, he lays it down and says, "I framed my favorite of the two of us. I keep it beside my bed."

"I saw it after bunko." I blink at him. "Why, Sonny? After so many years, why would you have our picture by your bed?"

"When my last marriage ended, I realized how cynical I'd become." His eyes flick to the window. His jaw tightens. "The things you see in a war will do that to you. And then the hospital and rehab…two divorces. I started thinking a lot about that time in my life. Our time." Returning his focus to me, he tucks a strand of hair behind my ear and says, "The picture reminds me something pure can exist in this world. We had it, Al, you and me. The real thing. The right love at the wrong time."

"Oh, Sonny." I crumble inside. Cupping his face in my hands, I kiss him softly, briefly, closing my eyes when he kisses me back.

The years melt away, the questions, the pain, the anger. There's only us again. Two kids against the world. The copper-haired boy with the teasing eyes, the defiant girl with the flower in her hair.

Chair legs scrape the floor. He stands, pulling me to my feet along with him, his mouth still on mine. Our bodies press together. I feel his hands slide into my hair.

I don't know how we end up in his bedroom, who closes and locks the door, who takes the first step toward the bed. So many years since the last time, but they don't matter now; they don't exist. Our breaths mingle like they did before; the murmured sounds of longing are the same, the lips on my face, my throat, my neck, are so familiar, so sweet.

He slides my shirt over my head. I open my eyes to undo his buttons.

The diamond in my engagement ring reflects the lamplight, blinding me. I blink to clear my vision.

Lowering my hands from his chest, I scoot away from Sonny, from his mouth and his hands and his memories. We stare into each other's eyes, and he's no longer that idealistic young man with a lifetime stretching ahead of him, and I'm not the free-spirited girl with limitless dreams.

I lean against the headboard. "I can't."

"I know." He moves to sit beside me, and when I look down at my left hand, his gaze follows mine. "You really do love him."

I nod, and tears rise again as I look at him. "But I love you, too. Is that possible?"

He touches my cheek. "You love who I was. I'm not that person anymore. Too much has happened."

I look at the photo on his nightstand. "That boy's still in you, Sonny. I see him sometimes."

He reaches for the frame. "And I still see her in you. But tell me, Al, who was in your head when we were kissing just now? Me as I am now, or me as I was then?"

I press my lips together, unable, unwilling, to answer.

"I'll be honest," he says. "When I closed my eyes, this is who I saw." He touches the photograph. "The young girl who believed in me and put me first when no one else did. The girl who thought I could do anything I set my mind to."

I realize that's what drew the two of us together so long ago. Our belief in one another. The fact that we each loved and accepted the other unconditionally. Sonny didn't expect me to prove anything to him, like my father did. And, unlike his parents, I made him feel strong and capable and important. In each other, we found what was missing in our lives.

While I pull my shirt back on, he returns the frame to the nightstand. Then he wraps his arms around me and, together, we lie back against the pillows. I listen to the beat of his heart for a minute. Two. Now's the time, I know it, but the words won't come. *Why did you leave me? What happened?*

"I would've held you back, Al," Sonny says, as if he heard my thoughts. He strokes my hair. "Just like your dad said I would."

I glance up at him. "He told you that?"

His forehead lifts. "That and a whole lot more. And he was right. You had a plan. I didn't have the faintest idea what to do with my life."

Sickened to think my father would make Sonny feel he wasn't good enough for me, I sit up. "That isn't true. We could've found our way."

"Maybe. But do you really think you would've accomplished all you have if we'd stayed together? You were sixteen years old, Al. Sixteen. Nick's age."

"So you're saying you left me because of my dad? Just like

213

that? Without a word, just disappeared one morning and never contacted me again?"

"It was more than your dad."

"Tell me, then. Do you have any idea how long I've wondered? I went to sleep in your arms then woke up the next morning alone. You'd vanished off the face of the earth. Can you even imagine how panicked I was? How worried I was about you?"

"I'm sorry. I didn't want that."

"Well, I was. Not to mention how betrayed and embarrassed I felt. And angry."

"Now, that I *was* counting on."

"What?" Angry all over again, I stand. "You wanted to sleep with me, piss me off and make me feel like a fool?"

"Whoa, now. Calm down and let me explain. Remember the day before we left for Woodstock? How quiet I was? You kept asking me what was wrong."

"I do remember. What *was* wrong?"

He gets up, goes to a bureau, opens a drawer and looks through it a moment. Then he takes something out – a paper – and brings it to me.

Sitting at the edge of the bed with Sonny beside me, I stare at the date on the draft notice, then read the words beneath. The message still holds enough power to sink my heart, as I know it would've thirty-six years ago.

"It came in the mail the day before we took off for Woodstock. Scared me shitless. Made me angry, too, that my country expected me to risk my life in a war that didn't make sense. That they'd expect anyone to do that."

Laying the letter in my lap, I look across at him. "Why didn't you do something?"

"Like what?"

"I don't know. Go to Canada. Anything."

"Don't think that didn't cross my mind. But only for a second. Right or wrong, I knew I had to go. This is my home, not Canada. And I had buddies over there."

I'm shaking. Finally, finally, I'm learning the truth, the answers to the questions that have haunted me so many years. "You should've told me. I would've waited for you, you know that."

"That's why I *didn't* tell you. Because I knew you'd wait. And while you did, you would've put your life on hold. Made it your mission to bring me home even if you had to storm the White House as an army of one to do it." His head tilts to one side, his expression filled with the affection of all he remembers about me. "Am I right?"

I press my lips together, trying to keep all I'm feeling from rushing out of me. Guilt and regrets. Relief and forgiveness. And sorrow so vast my heart could explode. "Yes, I would've tried. I remember how determined I could be. But—"

"At first, I planned to tell you. I went to your house. You weren't home, but your dad was."

"You told Dad?" If my father kept this from me, I'll have one more thing I can't forgive.

"No, I didn't tell him, but like I said, he told *me* a thing or two." Sonny's smile is sad. "How I wasn't right for you. How my life was going nowhere fast while you had a chance at scholarships to more than one university."

I shake my head. "God, he could be so arrogant. He was terrible to say all that to you. And wrong. Those were his plans for me, not mine."

"He was just being a concerned father. He had your best

interests at heart, Al. I admit I don't like the approach your dad took with me, but now that I'm older, I understand why he said what he did. He didn't want you to limit yourself or settle for less than you were capable of having."

"And you were less?" I hand him back the letter, dig my fingers into my palms, my entire body rebelling against that statement. "I wouldn't have been *settling*. God, I can't believe he could say those things to you. You were just a boy, and he tried to make you feel like a loser. Like you weren't good enough. I would have been happy staying at home and going to junior college while you worked and saved for trade school. Or what if I'd gone away to school and you followed me? You worked construction. You could've found a job anywhere."

Sonny takes my hand. "He was right to want you to forget about me."

"Quit saying that."

"Without me around, didn't you do all those things he said you would? All the things you told me way back then that you *wanted* to do?"

"Most of them. I put myself through school without his money, too." My chest feels tight. "And I didn't do the one thing that was most important to me. I didn't share my life with you. Who can say everything would've been more difficult, or that I'd have been less successful, if we'd stayed together? You can't convince me I wouldn't have done just as well for myself." Better, I think. I would have Sarah. We both would. "Maybe the route would've been a different one, but so what?"

"Regardless of your dad, *I* didn't want you waiting for me and worrying while I was over there getting shot at. How would you have survived it if I didn't make it through?"

A sigh shudders out of me. If he *had* died in the war and I found out all these years later, would that have been any easier?

"I must've tried a thousand times to tell you before we went to Woodstock, but I just couldn't," Sonny continues. "After we got there, I didn't want to blow the weekend, so I thought I'd wait until our last night. Then you told me about your dreams of going to school and having your own business, of being Mrs. Sonny McGraw some day, and I knew what I had to do."

He smiles. "We were two very different people, Al. With two different kinds of futures ahead of us. Your dad was hard on me, but he made me see the truth about that." His throat shifts. "I convinced myself I had to leave in a way that'd make you so pissed at me that you'd never want to lay eyes on me again. You were a stubborn little thing. If I'd told you the truth, you wouldn't have given up on me."

He takes the letter, stands and returns it to the bureau drawer, then says, "I talked myself out of leaving a couple of times, especially after we made love, but I always came back to it as the only answer." Turning to me, he closes his eyes. "I thought, if I made it through and came home, I'd find you and make you forgive me."

"Why didn't you?" He opens his eyes and comes over to sit beside me again. I touch his leg. "Because of this?"

Blinking, he nods. "I was in bad shape for a long time. Not only physically. I didn't want you seeing me like that."

"It wouldn't have mattered to me," I say in a choked voice.

"I wanted more for you. And so much time had passed. By the time I got out of the hospital then rehab, it'd been years since we saw each other. I figured you were in school, maybe you'd even met someone else. I didn't want to disrupt your life and make a mess of things."

"Disrupt my life? Every time the phone rang, or the doorbell, I prayed it was you. For years, Sonny."

"I'm sorry. You can't imagine the things that went through my mind during that time. When I was in rehab, I knew this guy who had burns over most of his body and his face. When his fiancée showed up and saw him for the first time, she turned away."

I lift a hand to my throat.

"She gave him back his ring, said she couldn't go through life looking at him like that every day."

"That's the cruelest thing I've ever heard. Surely, you didn't think—"

"I knew you wouldn't turn away from me. I also knew that if I glimpsed any pity in your eyes, it would kill me. And you deserved a strong man at your side, not someone you'd have to take care of and feel sorry for."

"You are strong. I wouldn't have felt like that." When his hand lifts to my cheek, I lean into it.

"Everything I did...I was trying to do right by you. Even though I knew you'd be hurt by me leaving like I did, I thought it would be the best for you. But now, knowing about Sarah, I feel like I failed you, anyway. Both of you."

Seeing the tears in his eyes, I blink back mine. "How could you have known? We each did what we thought we had to do at the time."

My own statement startles me, but now that it's spoken, I know it's true. Sonny left me out of love, not selfishness. At eighteen, life forced him to make a hard choice, and he did the best he could.

I forgive Sonny.

Now, if only I could find a way to forgive myself.

CHAPTER 15

*A*fter talking all night, Sonny and I sit down with Nick the next morning at the picnic table outside the house. They're side by side, with me across from them.

I prop my forearms on the table and lean forward. "We've been debating what the best thing for you would be, Nick. I'd love for you to come home and live with me in Portland. I want that very much. But it has to be what you want, too."

Sonny smoothes his mustache. "And nothing would make me happier than for you to live here with me. You could spend the summer helping me with the farm and we'd continue those riding lessons, like I promised. Then, come fall, we'd sign you up for school. It's a lot smaller than you're used to, I think there's only about twenty or so kids in your class, but it'll make it that much faster for you to get to know everybody." When I clear my throat and give him a look, he adds, "But I agree with Al. It has to be right for you."

Nick chews his lower lip and squirms. "So what'd you decide?"

"We didn't." Sonny and I exchange a bemused glance. "We're having some trouble with that."

"So we thought we'd ask you," Sonny explains.

Nick's expression clearly indicates that this is something new—adults asking his opinion about what's best for him. He stops bothering his lip, then looks from Sonny to me and back again. "Well, I've been thinking about it."

I hold my breath.

"The thing is, since I don't know anyone in Portland, I'm really gonna be bored there this summer. And when I get bored, stuff happens." He blushes.

Disappointment stings behind my eyes. Still, Nick's frankness both touches and amuses me.

"And, no offense, Ally," he continues, "but I don't really like working at the café all that much."

"None taken."

To Sonny's credit, he refrains from looking smug.

"I think I'd like working here with Sonny and learning to ride and work on the farm."

"I understand." And I do. But it still hurts to know that after I've grown to love him so much, I have to let him go now.

"But…" Nick faces Sonny. "Only twenty kids in my class?" He winces. "That's not many to choose from for friends. What if I don't like any of them, or they don't like me? School would really suck."

Sonny is the one who looks disappointed now. "There's no reason you wouldn't fit right in."

Nick appears doubtful. "I'm guessing there's no hockey league close by I could join?"

"The closest would be in Amarillo," Sonny answers. "And that'd be a lot of driving back and forth for practice and games."

Nick turns to me. "How about I live with Sonny during the summers and with you during the school year until I graduate? Then we could all get together over the holidays. Warren, too."

Sonny glances at me. He clears his throat.

"I like that idea," I say cautiously, dreading the possibility of another debate.

"Me, too." Sonny's mouth curves up at one side. He chuckles. "Warren might want to have a say in the holiday part, though."

I bite back a smile. "I'm sure we can work something out."

"So." Nick beams. "I don't have to go back?"

"I guess you're staying here until mid-August," I answer.

His smile slowly fades. "Are you still leaving today?"

"I'll wait until tomorrow morning, so I can get an earlier start." And some sleep.

Sonny slaps a hand to the table and says, "Okay, then. It's a plan."

We smile at each other. "Okay, then," I echo.

A weight lifts from my heart. If I had wings, I'd fly.

I spend a good part of the afternoon shopping for dinner groceries. To find everything I need requires a drive to Amarillo. I want to cook something special tonight, something we'll all enjoy, to celebrate our decision and the family we've become. An untraditional family, yes, but one with a bond already so tight, I feel the security of it like a warm hug around me. I hope Nick feels it, too.

We dine on wild mushroom soup, wilted spinach salad, skewered grilled shrimp and beef with anchovy butter. Afterward, I give Sonny Sarah's journals to read. "They're

Nick's but he shared them with me. He said you could read them, too."

"Thanks." Sonny holds the books as if they might break, his jaw tense, his eyes sad. "You sure you're finished with them?"

"No, but that's okay. Nick can bring them to me at the end of the summer." I stare at the ground. "I need some distance from them right now. It kills me to read them. Sarah didn't have the picture-perfect family life I imagined for her when I placed her for adoption."

"I doubt few kids do, Al. Adopted or not."

"But a lot of her bitterness was aimed at me." I nod at the journals. "Read them. She blamed me for giving her up. It's as simple as that."

"I hope you don't blame yourself. You were right when you said you did what you thought was best at the time. Just like I did."

"I know. I keep reminding myself of that." I blow out a weary breath. "But sometimes forgiveness doesn't come easy."

At the motel, I pack and call Teena. She assures me she's handling things.

"I want you to start interviewing for a couple more part-timers as soon as possible," I tell her.

"Before you get back?"

"If you can fit it in. I trust your judgement." About most things, anyway. I wouldn't trust her to color my hair.

"May I ask *why* you're finally hiring more help?"

"I'm going to need some more time off after I get home. I'm

leaving town for a wedding and a honeymoon. A *long* honeymoon. Mine."

She shrieks. "It's about time. Does Warren know?"

"He will in a few minutes." After she stops squealing, I say, "Hey, still no lisp. Does that mean Reid remains in the picture?"

She laughs. "I'm not letting him out of it. If I have my way, you're gonna be my stepmother-in-law one of these days."

I consider that and realize I wouldn't mind it. Not one bit.

After Teena's all talked out, I call Warren.

"Hi, honey," I say when he answers.

"Hi yourself. You sound chipper. What's up?"

"I'm coming home."

To you. Where I belong.

CHAPTER 16

Sonny stands on the porch watching Nick and me say goodbye in the driveway.

"With me staying here this summer," Nick says, trying to sound encouraging, "you won't have to worry about him passing out in the yard on bunko nights and staying there till morning."

Snickering, we both turn to the porch. "That's a load off my mind."

Nick reaches down and ruffles Sly's fur. "Watch out for Crow on your way back. And for dogs. Especially at carnivals."

I smirk at him. "I'm taking a different route home. A shorter one."

"Good idea."

"I'll call you tonight when I stop." I stoop to pet Sly, too, then glance up. "Thanks, Nick."

He frowns. "For what?"

For bringing me my daughter. For making me a grandmother. For helping me discover that the free-spirited girl I used to be still lives inside me. For leading me back to Sonny and the answers I needed to move on.

I smile at him and stand. "I wouldn't know where to begin, much less end." I open the car door. "Next time I see you, I'll be a married woman."

"You sure you don't want to wait until I get back and throw a big bash? I hear weddings are the best place to meet hot women."

I cross my arms and smirk at him. "I think we'll skip the hot women and just limit the ceremony to Warren and me."

"Tell him hi."

"I will."

We stare at each other. I guess I don't hide my emotions well because he says, "Hey, you can listen to Janis and Harry all the way to Portland with no complaints this time."

"I'll miss you more than I'd miss them, believe me." Laughing, I tap my foot. Leaving him is even more difficult than I expected. "Be good."

"I'll try."

"Try to give up the cigarettes, too, okay? It's a nasty habit."

"You've told me a million times."

"Listen to your grandfather. Be careful on the horses. And on the machinery."

"Jeez." He shakes his head. "You're starting to sound like Mom."

Our eyes meet, hold. Mine fill with tears. His do, too. I step toward him and we hug each other until he starts to fidget with embarrassment.

I step back. "I love you."

Glancing down at his feet, he says, "I love you, too," then

clears his throat. His relief is obvious when Sly starts barking on the porch. "I, uh, better get him some water."

"Sure."

Sonny starts down the steps, passing Nick on the way up. He carries Sarah's journals. "I'm not going to say goodbye," he says when he stops in front of me.

"How about 'until next time'?"

"Until next time, it is." His eyes shine as he lifts the journals. "I finished these last night."

"All of them?"

"Stayed up half the night reading." He hands them to me. "I couldn't put them down. Our daughter was quite a girl."

"Yes." Swallowing past the lump in my throat, I turn and put the journals into the car.

"You said you didn't read to the end?"

I shake my head, too emotional all of a sudden, too vulnerable.

"Do me a favor. Stop at the café on the way out. Buy a cup of coffee from Hank and at least read the last entry." When I frown at him, he says, "Promise me."

What's with the men in my life and all these promises they ask of me? "Okay. I promise." One last time, I turn toward the car and scan the interior to make sure Nick hasn't left anything in there.

"Make pit stops along the way, Al. It's a long drive alone."

"I'll take my time. I think I'm going to make a side trip to Walla Walla and see my parents for a day." I face him again and feel myself blush. "I guess I want to start my new life with a completely clean slate. You know, forgive and forget?" I shrug. "Well, forgive, anyway."

One brow rises. "I'd say to tell them hello, but it might not go over too well."

"I'll tell them, anyway. It's time they got over a few things, too."

Clearing his throat, Sonny takes off his hat, his eyes steady on mine. "I wish you and Warren the best."

"Thanks." Tilting my head, I squint at him. "Are you going to give Cindy Cobly a chance?"

His skeptical smirk isn't all that convincing. "I can't imagine why she'd want to give *me* a chance."

"I can. And believe me, she *does* want to. I know the look of a woman in love."

I glance to the porch where Nick plays with Sly.

"I'll take care of him," Sonny says.

"I know you will."

"Al—"

I meet his eyes. Staring back at me are all the same emotions I'm feeling. The same memories I'll always cherish. The same gratitude that we found one another again.

Sonny's lips part. "I—"

Lifting my fingers to his mouth, I nod. "I know."

When he opens his arms, I step into them.

CHAPTER 17

February 5, 2005

Dear Diary,

It's been a while, I know. I haven't felt like writing. The doctor gave me bad news. The cancer is back. This time for good, most likely.

I've done a lot of thinking in the past weeks. About Nick mostly, but also about my parents, my life. What would I change? If anything had been any different, I might not have had Nick, and I can't imagine any happiness without him. And, so, maybe I wouldn't change anything. Except that I would've spent even more time with him, laughed more, eaten more ice cream, watched less television. Oh, and spent less time being angry and bitter.

Which brings me to the mystery parents. The mystery mother, especially.

I've been thinking about that time I drove to Portland to see her. There are things about her I didn't tell you before. I was too conflicted about my feelings. For instance, how beautiful her smile was, how it was so wide that it wrinkled the sides of her eyes. About the emotion I recognized in them when she looked at my hair. About the love I heard in her voice when she said the words *my daughter.*

I don't blame her anymore.

So, why can't I tell her that? Even now, I can't bring myself to pick up the phone, or even to write her a letter. I tell myself it might be too difficult for her to hear that I am probably dying. Maybe everything's better left as is, so she can continue searching the eyes of other women who look like they might be her baby girl grown up. So the hope I saw on her face that day at the café can last forever.

She loved me. I don't need to hear her say it. I knew it when she looked at me and our fingers touched.

At different times in our lives, we faced the same decisions. She made hers and I made mine. In the end, we both chose wisely.

So I'm sending this message out into the universe with the hope it will somehow find her, and she will hear it in her heart:

Mother…Even before I saw your face or heard your voice or touched you, a part of me always felt a connection. I understand why you did what you did, and though I struggled with resentment over it for a long time, the resentment is gone, and I forgive you. I have had some wonderful things in my life. I hope you have, too. I hope you are happy, and that your life is rich and full.

Your daughter

~Sarah

J stare a long time at both Sarah's journal and the letter I wrote after reading the last entry. Finally, I sign my name, lay the pen aside and take off my glasses. Folding the page, I slide it into the envelope, along with Sarah's photographs, then place everything in my purse.

I take the pen to the prune-faced man behind the register. Hank, I suppose. We never formally met. "Thanks for letting me borrow this. And the paper."

"No problem," he says. "Come back and see us."

I tilt my head to the side. "Maybe, I will."

It's windy and cool outside. A cloud hides the sun.

I climb behind the wheel of the Beamer, then drive out of the Cowgirl Café parking lot. Once on the highway, I look in my rearview mirror at my last glimpse of Mesquite Bend and think of Sonny's farm....

"All that land...Miles and miles with no buildings, just pastures and trees. Man...and the sky, it's so blue. And clean...all those fat cows...and horses...Christ, I love horses."

I laugh aloud, hearing Sonny's young voice in my mind, saying those words a long time ago.

I imagine him now, leaving Nick and Sly roughhousing in the yard while he goes in to gather the photos we left on his kitchen table. He places them back into the shoe box then carries it to his bedroom. There, he takes the framed photograph of the two of us off his nightstand, puts it into the box, too, and replaces the lid. The box goes on the top shelf of his closet.

When I'm home, I'll do the same with the photos of Sarah in

my purse and the letter I wrote to her. Tuck them into the album filled with pictures of Sonny and me, then put them away in the closet.

Away, but not forgotten.

Like the past I once wished I could forget, but now know I never can. Or should. The girl I used to be, the life she lived, is intertwined with the woman I am. I won't ever forget her. I won't forget the past, but I can accept it and the choices I made. I can move on, stronger and wiser because of them.

"Until next time," I whisper to the road behind me, then shift my gaze ahead. A ray of sunlight breaks through the clouds.

I think of Warren.

Dear Sarah,

I wish I'd had the chance to tell you these things.... You came from love, and I loved you so much. I've thought of you every day since I last held you in my arms. The hardest decision I ever made was to let you go

Thank you for sending Nick to me. You raised a fine young man. Sensitive. Bright. Strong. Knowing him has forced me to face things about myself I've avoided for too long. He has helped me find all that was missing in my life and made me aware of all the happiness and love that was already there, waiting for me to drink it in. I am proud of him. And of you. Of your strength and resilience. Of your courage and the loving mother you were. As long as we live, your father and I will protect and cherish and love your son. Through Nicholas, you set us all on a course back to one another. We are finally a family.

Goodbye, my beautiful daughter. I love you. You will live in my heart forever.

Your Mother,

Allyson

SNEAK PEEK OF WHAT I NEVER EXPECTED

Chapter 1

Like most children of my generation, I grew up eating balanced meals from the basic food groups. But in addition to the selections on the food pyramid chart, my grandmother, June Hester, spoon-fed me heaping helpings of her homegrown Texas legends – a colorful conglomeration of Bible verses (though she wasn't particularly religious), superstitious folklore (though she wasn't a flake), and her own vivid imagination (which she had in abundance). I called her Nanny, and because everyone else in Creed County did, I called my granddaddy Chick.

"Did you know I heard you before I ever laid eyes on your tiny pink face, Maggie Sue?"

I was only six-years-old when Nanny first told me the tale of my birth. It was a warm summer evening, and she, Chick and I were sitting on the front porch of our farmhouse. Beyond the pot-holed graveled road, darkness slowly swallowed an orange sun that clung to the edge of our neighbor's field.

"You was ten miles down the way," Nanny continued. "Out by Red Homer's place. Your Mama'd pulled your uncle Ned's old truck into the ditch alongside Red's land when the pain got too much for her."

"That can't be." I cozied up close to her padded body in the rocking chair. Her blouse smelled like baked bread, her hands like Jergen's lotion. "Ten miles is far. How could you hear me?"

Ribbons of smoke curled out of Chick's brown cigarette. "You came out screeching like a banshee, little girl," he said with a raspy chuckle.

Nanny's work-callused palm brushed hair from my forehead. "You cried out to me, Sugarbee. Called for me to save you. Guess you sensed your Mama wouldn't make it." She glanced away, her eyes glossy with tears that she quickly blinked back.

"If I'd been bigger, I would've saved Mama," I said, patting her leg.

"I know you would'a tried," answered Nanny with a sniff, smiling as she faced me again.

"So you heard me crying and went running to find me?"

"Not 'til the blackbird came."

"The blackbird?"

"He flew by you and Leanne in that car and swallowed your wails."

I frowned and sat straighter. The rocking chair creaked. "But—"

"Chick was off working, and I was on my knees digging radishes in the garden when that bird landed on the barbed wire. He opened his beak and out come your squallin'."

Even at six, I didn't quite believe her tall tale. "My voice came out of a bird?" I asked.

"So she says," Chick muttered with a lift of one bushy brow. Flicking ash from the tip of his cigarette, he added, "Try as I might, I cain't get her to share what she drinks to bring on them delusions."

Scowling at him, Nanny said, "Don't listen to that old fool. What I'm sayin's true. Birds are angels on earth, Sugarbee."

I thought about that while tracing a fingertip across the raised blue veins lining the top of her hand. June bugs buzzed around the yellow porch light and summer scents hung heavy in the air: the sweet, ripe aroma of peaches in the crate by the door, freshly mowed grass, the tang of Chick's burning tobacco. Out by the road, fireflies flickered. "Did Uncle Ned hear, too?" I asked.

"Ned was off fightin' the war then," Nanny said of her only son, my mother's older brother.

"Over in 'Nam," Chick added, a ragged edge to his voice.

"Like my daddy?"

They glanced at each other. Nanny nodded.

"How did you know it was me crying?" I asked.

"Kinfolk know kinfolk, Maggie." My hand slid up Nanny's arm, and beneath my touch, goosebumps erupted on her skin. Her sharp blue eyes met mine and looked deep. "I heard your Mama in your cries, heard my own self, too. And my mama before me."

GET A FREE NOVELLA - SUBSCRIBE TO MY NEWSLETTER

*N*ever miss a new release by signing up for my newsletter at http://www.jenniferarcher.com/newsletter/. When you do, I'll send you a link to download my novella, "Take a Little Risk."

I'll never spam you and will only reach out when there is important information to share or a new release.

I can't wait to connect with you!

ALSO BY JENNIFER ARCHER

WOMEN'S FICTION

Sandwiched

Off Her Rocker

YOUNG ADULT FICTION

Through Her Eyes

The Shadow Girl

CHILDREN'S PICTURE BOOK

A Zack Attack: The Shenanigans of a Picky Eater

NON-FICTION

Happiness Rehab: 8 Creative Steps to a More Joyful Life

ROMANTIC COMEDY

Make A Little Magic Series

Spark A Little Flame (Book 1)

Dream A Little Dream (Book 2)

ABOUT THE AUTHOR

Jennifer Archer is the author of numerous fiction and non-fiction works. Her novels have been nominated for Romance Writers of America's prestigious Rita Award and Romantic Times Bookclub's Reviewer's Choice Award. In 2013, the Texas Library Association selected her debut young adult novel, Through Her Eyes, for their first spirit of Texas Reading Program – Middle School, and for the TAYSHAS High School reading list. Jennifer enjoys teaching creativity and creative writing workshops. She also writes and edits for clients through her business, Archer Editing & Writing Services (archereditingandwriting.com). She lives in Texas with her husband and three dogs.

If you want to read more about Jennifer or if you're curious about when her next book will come out, please visit her website at: http://www.jenniferarcher.com, where you can sign up to receive email notifications about new releases.

Connect with Jennifer on social media, visit her website, or email her.

facebook.com/Jennifer-Archer-159335414094711
twitter.com/jenniferarcher1
instagram.com/jenniferarcher01
bookbub.com/authors/jennifer-archer